Duncan Anderson

Scottish folk-lore

Duncan Anderson

Scottish folk-lore

ISBN/EAN: 9783744771498

Printed in Europe, USA, Canada, Australia, Japan

Cover: Foto ©Andreas Hilbeck / pixelio.de

More available books at **www.hansebooks.com**

Scottish Folk-Lore

BY

THE REV. DUNCAN ANDERSON, M.A.

AUTHOR OF "THE LAYS OF CANADA," ETC.

Eheu! fugaces labuntur anni.

TORONTO

GEORGE N MORANG & COMPANY LIMITED

1899

TO THEIR EXCELLENCIES,

The Earl and Countess of Aberdeen,

THIS HUMBLE WORK IS DEDICATED BY
SPECIAL PERMISSION ;
DEDICATED, IN ACKNOWLEDGMENT OF SELF-DENYING LABORS,
ON TWO CONTINENTS, TO PROMOTE
HUMAN HAPPINESS ;
IN ADMIRATION OF UNTIRING PERFORMANCE OF EVERY
PUBLIC AND PRIVATE DUTY ;
AND, ESPECIALLY, AS AN EXPRESSION OF THE
HEARTIEST SYMPATHY WITH THAT NOBLEST OF TASKS THAT THEY
HAVE CHOSEN AS PECULIARLY THEIR OWN—
TO BUILD UP AND FOSTER
AMONGST ALL, A HIGHER, A PURER, A HOLIER
BROTHERHOOD.

MONYMUSK, November, 1895.

DEAR MR. ANDERSON,

To be associated with any of your literary or other work, and more especially in the case of what cannot fail to be a very interesting narrative, would be agreeable to Lady Aberdeen and myself; therefore I cordially assent to your kind proposal regarding the dedication of your forthcoming book. With best wishes, I remain, very truly yours,

ABERDEEN.

CONTENTS.

CHAPTER I.

MY PINAFORE.

CHAPTER II.

SILLERTON AND ITS SURROUNDINGS.

CHAPTER III.

SILLERTON AND ITS NOTABILITIES.

CHAPTER IV.

THE DOMINIE.

CHAPTER V.

THE DOMINIE—CONTINUED.

CHAPTER VI.

THE DOMINIE MOUNTED.

CHAPTER VII.

A DISSOLVING VIEW.

CHAPTER VIII.

THE STICKIT LAWYER.

CHAPTER IX.

DOCTOR LOW'S WATCH LOST AND FOUND.

CHAPTER X.

HOW MARY MITCHELSON DISHED HER HUSBAND'S BROSE.

CHAPTER XI.

THE QUEEN'S SCOTCH AS SPOKEN IN SILLERTON.

CHAPTER XII.

JEAN BARDEN'S MILK FOR BABES.

CHAPTER XIII.

THE POOR PRIOR TO THE POOR LAWS.

CHAPTER XIV.

LICENSED BEGGARS, THE FATUOUS AND INSANE.

CHAPTER XV.

CONVIVIALITIES OF SILLERTON.

CHAPTER XVI.

OTHER SILLERTON AMUSEMENTS : THE SOCIETY OF GARDENERS.

CHAPTER XVII.

THE WARS OF THE ROSES.

CHAPTER XVIII.

PRACTICAL JOKERS AT WORK.

CHAPTER XIX.

THE WINNING LEG.

CHAPTER XX.

THE MINISTER'S CHRISTMAS DINNER.

CHAPTER XXI.

SILLERTON'S BURDENS.

CHAPTER XXII.

NON-INTRUSION.—THE NIGHT BEFORE THE BATTLE.

CHAPTER XXIII.

THE CULSALMOND RIOT.

CHAPTER XXIV.

LAST DAYS AT SCHOOL.

CHAPTER XXV.

CONCLUSION.—THE COMPETITION AND THE GOWN.

PREFATORY NOTE.

When I was first asked to write a few lines by way of introducing, particularly to the public of Ontario, the work of my old friend Duncan Anderson, I thought such an introduction totally unnecessary, more especially as the book is commended by the high authority of our late honored Governor-General the Earl of Aberdeen. As, however, it was represented to me that there might be some to whom the name of the author was unknown, who might attach some value to my judgment of his work, I consented.

Of the interest and value of these reminiscences there can be no question. The phases of Scottish life here represented are passing away. Railways, electric telegraphs, and newspapers are obliterating local peculiarities; and the language spoken by the common people fifty years ago will soon be almost unintelligible to their grandchildren. It is of the highest importance that there should be preserved some permanent memorial of those men and manners and ways of life which would otherwise be forgotten : and the author of this volume possesses high qualifications for the performance of such a work.

Of Highland blood, but educated amid Lowland surroundings ; a good scholar, as old Aberdeen men know well, with considerable poetical gifts, as his published verses testify, and with a memory quite marvellously retentive ; Mr. Anderson has no ordinary fitness for the work which he has here undertaken, and which, in the judgment of the present writer, he has accomplished with so much success. His sketches have all the accuracy of photographs, and yet they reflect, in no slight measure, the fine temper, the genial humor, the cultivated taste of their author. As an illustration of their historical value, reference may be made to the account of the Culsalmond Riot, every detail of which may be verified from the newspapers of the period.

It is not quite easy for one who graduated along with the author at Aberdeen, about half a century ago, to read these sketches without emotions which cannot be shared by all their readers ; but I am greatly mistaken if I do not earn the gratitude of those who may be induced, by my words of appreciation, to make themselves acquainted with the contents of these pages.

WILLIAM CLARK.

Trinity University,
Toronto, June, 1899.

INTRODUCTION.

By these mysterious ties, the busy power
Of memory her ideal train preserves
Entire; or when they would elude her watch,
Reclaims their fleeting footsteps from the waste
Of dark oblivion.
—AKENSIDE.

THE late Dean Ramsay of Edinburgh, in the preface to his Reminiscences, says, "It is interesting to preserve national peculiarities which are passing away from us."

The remark is one that strikes with peculiar force every Scotchman, and as the years go by, and those who capped our best stories with some of their own, join the majority, the feeling deepens with us that the opportunities of preserving such peculiarities are indeed very materially lessening. Not much more than a decade of years has passed since I was invited to meet, at the house of an intimate friend, two or three acquaintances, formerly residents of Quebec, but whose lines had now fallen to them in other places.

We were all of us of that class, that, loving Scot-

1

land as it should be loved, enjoyed the pleasure of telling, and hearing told, the stories of our native land.

It need scarcely be remarked that the sma' hours were reached long before we thought of separating. Before, however, Auld Lang Syne was sung, the host remarked, "What a pity that these stories that have been told here to-night should be lost! Could a stenographer have been stationed within earshot, what an interesting paper might he have supplied to thousands of readers, and would not the object be thus gained of rendering imperishable what after all, may, in a few years, be difficult, perhaps impossible, to recall?"

This remark struck us all, and we then agreed, that, if ever a convenient season came, we would put our heads and pens together, and endeavor to do, each in his way, what the reporter might have done for us.

That convenient season, however, never came, and when I looked around me only lately, I was painfully reminded that it could now never come. Impelled by a feeling of regret, I resolved to do alone, in a humble way, what might have been so much better done by us all. I felt like the subaltern under fire, who knows that, however unfit he may be, yet it is still his duty to lead on, when his superior officers have been laid low on the field of battle.

But how to perform my duty in the best way, I was at a loss to determine. The mere stringing of anecdotes together did not take my fancy, and it would be difficult to follow in the footsteps of such men as Ramsay and O'Rell, without provoking a comparison that might be at least unpleasant, and I had, in consequence, to relinquish all idea of relating almost anything except what was mainly my own.

Another way then lay open to me, for which I had, I believed, one special qualification, and that way I adopted. So far as my recollection of individuals, and of circumstances connected with them, was concerned, memory never failed me. Like the musician whom two or three notes will often enable to repeat the almost forgotten melody, so, on recalling some acquaintance of my early years, the outline, at first only dim and indistinct, becomes gradually clothed with a flood of light, and the minutest traits of appearance and character, and life and sayings, stand out boldly as if I had been contemplating them but yesterday. This decided me. I had no intention of creating characters to suit my story, if indeed story it might be called, for like Canning's needy knife-grinder, I might say—

"Story? God bless your honor, I have none to tell, Sir,"

but there were men and women that I had known

nearly a half century ago, and these I would call as
witnesses, and make them once more tell their own
tale. In telling it, they would, at the same time,
give a faithful picture of a quiet Aberdeenshire
village and parish, about forty or fifty years ago.

Why I have used on my title-page, "From Pinafore to Gown," is readily enough explained. I
quickly found that the materials on hand would
soon swell to the proportions of a somewhat un-
wieldy volume, and I imagined that what I recollected of Sillerton from boyhood till I entered
college, would be sufficient, in size and quality, to
test my chances of success as a faithful historian of
folk-lore.

I have contrived to throw what must prove a very
flimsy veil over places and individuals, but I feel
persuaded that if any one finds himself or his friends
portrayed in these humble pages, the recognition of
the likeness will not, under any circumstances, be
accompanied with pain.

I may add that I have attempted to sketch Sillertonians, certainly not as they should have been, but
such as they were; if I fail to interest the reader, I
must pay the penalty of failure; if success crowns
my efforts, I shall not, in that case, present my
P. P. C. card.

D. A.

SCOTTISH FOLK-LORE.

CHAPTER I.

MY PINAFORE.

My eyes are dim with childish tears,
  My heart is idly stirred;
For the same sound is in my ears
  Which in those days I heard.
            —WORDSWORTH.

PINAFORE, did I say? Yes, it was a blue pinafore that I wore. Whether it was intended for ornament or use, or perhaps for both purposes, I cannot now well say, but yet the color and pattern are as well stamped upon memory's page as if I had worn the garment but yesterday.

And yet sixty years, more or less, make a long telescope through which an old man observes a pinafore that he wore when his wavy locks hung in ringlets over his shoulders. Sixty years, more or less, did I say? Ah! certainly, not less, not less. I like truth under any circumstances, although

5

sometimes it may be a bitter pill to swallow, when swallowing is in order.

But then, what of more? Well, I feel comparatively young still. Let me hear the whirr of a hardwood partridge amongst the maple branches in the dear month of October, and then what eye is brighter, what foot is fleeter, than mine? Let a north shore salmon, fresh from the icy seas of Labrador, get upon my line, and is it a feeble hand that guides him through swirl and pool to a quiet corner, or a feeble voice that joins in the joyous whoop that my Indian gives as he lays the glittering beauty on the pebbly shore?

But yet the silken ringlets went long ago, when my mother, with tears coursing down her cheeks, cut them all away, and selected only one to fill that locket that has hung unworn now for nearly fifty years. But there are curls yet; alas! not everywhere, but yet in fair abundance, and with a few threads of silver amongst them, and making them look just as if a sprinkling of snowflakes had touched them gently amidst the frolics of the Christmas time. Not less then, but say more.

But writing of snowflakes reminds me of the first time that any one seemed to notice that Father Time had taken liberties with me. A daughter who had spent a few years in a foreign land, and who never failed to break down when the choir of the church where she worshipped sung Payne's beautiful hymn, "Home, Sweet Home!" sent us unexpected tidings of an intended visit. The wintry morning was bitterly cold; the loud whistle of the approaching train had, a few minutes before, intimated its arrival; the old flag was run up to the mast-head; the merry jingling of sleigh-bells was heard, and our long absent one was soon folded in our arms. There were no dry eyes there, for do they not overflow both at the touch of joy as well as of sorrow?

Looking at me through her blinding tears, she said, suiting the action to the word, "Father, let me brush the snow away from your beard." "Ah, Janie, that snow can never be brushed away. It is God's harbinger of the winter of age. It has come to stay."

To return to my pinafore. I cannot describe exactly the pattern, yet I could swear to it among a thousand. Like the "willow" pattern on our own dinner sets, so the "pinafore" pattern must have come down to us for many generations, and for aught that I know very probably suggested the idea to the artist who had the honor of designing the Star-spangled Banner. Why I so clearly recollect that pinafore I have an idea. There seems to be, at times, small hooks that pin things firmly to memory, and there was one in this instance.

It was a beautiful Sunday morning in spring. We were all dressed accordingly. Accordingly means ready for church, the service in which commenced in those days at the very reasonable hour of noon. Father had arrived from a distance the night before, and had brought small presents for the little ones. Mine was a somewhat peculiar imitation watch, not in nickel or tin, as nowadays, but in some species of delfware that shone like old gold. With this stuck in a pocket put in my new pinafore evidently for the occasion, I strolled out to the churchyard, which lay just behind the village, my object being to gather a bouquet of gowans, and to enjoy myself generally—that is, with such decorum as the Sabbath, or at least Scottish parents, demanded of little folks in Scotland in those days.

Wandering among the grassy mounds that marked the places where

" The rude forefathers of the hamlet slept,"

and gathering my bouquet of daisies and primroses, I found myself at the low window of the cobbler's shop which looked out upon the churchyard.

I had never looked in at that window before. Out of it I had often looked, for Sandy Simms, the village shoemaker, and I, notwithstanding the disparity of ages, were good friends. Sandy loved to tell a good story, and to hear one as well, and when the hobbledehoys came to have their shoes patched, or to get irons fastened upon the toes of their heavy boots in preparation for a game of football, for which pastime the village boys of Sillerton were famous over at least a dozen parishes, Sandy's tongue and rozetty ends kept good time together. What the forte was that charmed the rustics I cannot now remember; there must, however, have been no small art displayed, seeing that the souter's shop almost rivalled the blacksmith's smithy, while we little folks, if we did not quite understand the gist of all we heard, yet never failed to show unbounded delight, by opening not only ears, but also eyes and mouth, at the souter's eloquence. Personally, then, if, indeed, an urchin of my years could lay claim to a distinct and separate personality, I owed Sandy no grudge. His tongue had never suggested to me that it was time for small boys to be jogging homewards, nor had his elison ever expedited my movements in that direction. On the other hand the genial souter had been kindness itself personified.

What then could have prompted me to do anything to hurt the feelings or property of my friend I am unable to say. That I should at that moment,

in that quiet churchyard, on that calm and beautiful Sunday morning, draw out of my pocket that
newly-acquired watch and with it coolly and deliberately, as if from malice prepense, break a pane
of glass in the cobbler's window, has proved to be a
problem as hard of solution as the squaring of the
circle has been to the long-baffled mathematician.

Was it the result of pride in the possession of that
spurious imitation of a timekeeper; did convenience
snug stir up the treacherous inclination; or was it
possible that the very deil himself whispered in the
ear of my heart to prove my manhood by breaking
the window of the souter's workshop?

I need not say how soon remorse came. I felt
that day in church as if I had not merely broken a
pane of glass, but as if I had murdered the souter
himself. I could scarcely say my short prayer that
night, and for days after, my punishment was almost
greater than I could bear. Oh! dear Tom Hood! you
must, when a boy, have cracked some friendly cobbler's window unprovoked, else never could you
have written these lines—

> " O Heaven ! to think of their white souls,
>   And mine so black and grim !
> I could not share in childish prayer,
>   Nor join in evening hymn : ·
> Like a Devil of the Pit I seem'd
> 'Mid holy Cherubim ! "

For months after I would have walked a Scotch mile rather than pass that wretched window with the patched pane of glass in it, and I never had the courage to enter Sandy's workshop again. Alas! it is conscience that makes cowards of us all. What wonder then was it that my little ears ceased to listen to the old stories that I had so often heard before from the eloquent lips of the kindly souter, or that I had never forgotten the blue pinafore that I had worn on that eventful and sadly-to-be-lamented Sunday morning?

CHAPTER II.

SILLERTON AND ITS SURROUNDINGS.

How still the morning of the hallowed day;
Mute is the voice of rural labor ; hushed
The ploughboy's whistle and the milkmaid's song.
—GRAHAME.

SILLERTON, after all, was a strange name for a quiet, impecunious village, or rather quiet country parish. In fact the godfathers and godmothers of that ilk must have been wags in their way, and given the name on the *Lucus a non lucendo* principle, for siller did not lie about promiscuously in the village, or in the parish either. It is true that there were considerable operations in timber carried on in the neighborhood, but these, beyond giving a miserable wage to a few men, filled the pockets of the laird only, who knew well how to earn and how to keep his profits.

There was also a distillery that manufactured a limited quantity of the genuine mountain dew, but very limited that quantity must have been, seeing that the manager, when trying to sell his goods one market day to a jolly farmer who was noted for the quantity and quality of his liquor, and being told that unless he lowered his prices he might shut up shop altogether, at once retorted—"Na, na, man; as lang's we hae the same manager and the same partners we are quite capable of drinking the haill browst oursels." It is almost needless to say that the bibulous manager got an order on the spot.

Sillerton then was somewhat like Rob Rorison's bonnet. "It was not the bonnet, but the head that was in it," and so with Sillerton: it was not so much the locality that we should desire to place before the readers as the notabilities that lived there.

Once, on questioning an old crone, on the deck of an arriving Quebec liner, what part of Scotland she hailed from, the answer came without a moment's hesitation, "Sooser than Golspie, at anyhoo," Golspie being rather in proximity to John o' Groat's. Here we shall be more precise, Sillerton lay on a low valley on Donside, and in full view of the last peak of the Grampian range that overlooks the whole Buchan district, and recalls to our memory the well-known line or lines, often quoted on the east coast :—

> "Tap o' Noth and Bennachie
> Are twa landmarks o' the sea."

The village occupied a central position in the

parish, and was composed of about two dozen dwell-
ing-houses, an imposing church that very probably
once formed part of an ancient abbey, a good school
and schoolhouse, an excellent inn, where man and
beast could always command the best attention
possible, and the village store, where the guid wife
could exchange her butter, cheese, and eggs for
those creature comforts that warm alike the outer
and inner man. Add to these the meal mill,
the smithy, the carpenter's and the shoemaker's
workshops, and last, though not least, the famous
distillery, and you have a fair picture of Sillerton.

Ah! could I sweep away, as by magician's wand,
half a century of years; could I summon the old
villagers to return, and be as they once were, what
a shaking of dry bones would be in that old churchyard! What strange groups would pass along the
street; how quaint would appear their habiliments ;
how different from what the village man or maid
may now display!

Come, let us stand at the old iron gate that sep-
arates the village of the living from the homes of the
dead. Closed during the busy week, if indeed Sillerton was ever busy, it opens only on the day of rest,
to admit the worshippers to the house of God, or to
wander, perchance, for a brief space until the bell
proclaims the hour of prayer,—wander, we say,

amongst the countless mounds that mark the last resting-places of departed ones whom we never knew, and of some, too, whom we knew right well and whose memory, yet fresh and green, may bring a tear to the eye and sometimes, alas! a pang to the heart.

A framed board, attached to the church wall, is eagerly scanned by the gathering crowd, anxious to learn what matters of public interest are there recorded for the benefit of the good folks of Sillerton: while near by stands a stone, somewhat elevated above the ground, on which the beadle will by and by take his stand, at the "skailin' o' the kirk," and, in stentorian tones, announce the coming events of importance that are on the tapis for the week, perhaps ending with the pleasant announcement that Jamie Robb, the pedler, will hold a riffle of Carse o' Gowrie apples, handkerchiefs, and tobacco, on Wednesday evening next, at the farm of Flechneuk, and closing, very likely, with the remark that there would be a dance after the raffle.

How strange! some will say, and this too, in Sabbath-keeping Scotland! Ah! fifty years hence old men may be telling to astonished listeners that they often heard ministers reading notices from the pulpit that had long ere then found their proper place among the advertisements of the daily or weekly newspaper.

But, hush! the bell has ceased tolling; the wanderers among the green mounds are hurrying nearer the church door; while Dawvid Dunbar, the beadle, looms in sight, walking slowly from the manse gate towards the church, and carrying in his hand the large pulpit Bible, while behind him, with equal pace, but with infinite dignity, rolls along the Reverend Robert Fordyce, M. A., minister of the parish of Sillerton.

The crowd that till then had been enjoying the usual "crack," file in rapidly as the steps of the beadle and parson draw near the iron gate, the last to enter being a couple that had availed themselves of the opportunity that the morning's walk afforded of whispering murmurings of love to each other, and who now enter the sacred edifice by different doors, for, strange to say, there were at least half a dozen side doors in the church of Sillerton.

At last, all have found their places in the different seats set apart for the parishioners; the principal door is swung to upon its massive hinges; there is a moment or two of almost painful silence; and then, rising majestically in his plain but seemly pulpit, the minister of Sillerton, in slow and solemn tones, opens the service of the sanctuary in the well-known phrase—"Let us worship God by singing to His praise in the Hundredth Psalm."

CHAPTER III.

SILLERTON AND ITS NOTABILITIES.

And the guid Culdees o' Sillerton
  Might plead for King Malcolm's repose,
Wha vow'd to Sanct Andrew, their haly house,
  For victory o'er his foes.
   "*The Devil's Stane o' Kemnay,*" *slightly altered.*

WE were interrupted in our description of Sillerton and its surroundings by the commencement of
public worship in the parish church. We shall now
resume our subject, and Sillerton once properly
located, as an American would probably put it, we
may now proceed to sketch a few of its notabilities.
There were, in those golden days, no dissenters, so
called, in the parish. Had Sillerton possessed a
Temple of Janus, the doors would undoubtedly have
been closed, and the janitor might have safely locked
them and become a Rip Van Winkle for a few
years without any dread of interruption to his
slumbers.

The only other place of worship, besides the parish church, was a small Episcopal chapel, once a

2

lapidary's workshop, with a unique history of its own, but now considerably remodelled, and almost covered with ivy, and showing a Maltese cross upon either gable, as if to indicate its now sacred character.

This building accommodated sufficiently a small number of the parishioners who still clung to the Episcopal form of worship, and who, along with about a dozen aristocratic families who drove there from considerable distances around, waited upon the min-istrations of the Rev. William Walcott, M. A., well known for his Broad Church proclivities, an excel-lent scholar, an author (afterwards) of consider-able notability, and who, notwithstanding all these accomplishments, had yet the good sense to preach sermons that were never known to exceed fifteen minutes in the delivery.

The church of Sillerton, as has been said, was once probably part of an abbey, but the steeple, to which the church itself seemed a "lean-to," was of a much more ancient date, and was generally sup-posed to have been built by Malcolm Canmore, King of Scotland. Well it may be that Canmore was a first-class fighting man, but, judging from his at-tempt at building towers, he must, as an architect have proved a sad failure. We cannot, indeed, even with all our admiration for the great Malcolm, con-gratulate the ancient king upon the beauty of conception displayed, though certainly in durability of material used he takes the cake.

It is at least curious also that the tower of Sillerton church should have, in one respect—that is to say, in the precise and exact amount of overcharge or undercharge of price for value received—resembled the breeches of King Robert the Bruce. The latter were too dear, the former too cheap. Tradition has it that the king was somewhat stingy with the royal tailor—as the song says :—

> " In days when our King Robert rang,
>   His trews they cost but half a croon ;
> He said they were a groat ower dear,
>   And ca'd the tailor thief an' loon."

On the other hand, it has also been handed down that when the mason who built the tower of Sillerton had finished his work, and was on his way homewards, he looked back at the building and said, " Had I got a groat more I would have been satisfied." Groats must have been scarce in those days. Is it possible also that that dissatisfied mason had read the life of Hiram King of Tyre, who aided Solomon in his great work, and thereafter expressed anything but satisfaction with the return made by the Wise King ? Being a Scotchman, and likely an Aberdonian at that, this may have well been so, and the groat too little in the case of the tower builder was

much the same as the cities in Galilee that Hiram
so heartily despised.

Now in attempting to describe the notabilities of
Sillerton, I feel it slightly difficult to decide exactly
where to begin.   Are the greater or lesser lights to
come first ?

But, as we now stand facing the tower, the puzzle
seems solved by beginning at the right hand.

Poor old John Laing was not much of a notability,
and yet I could not consider a photo of Sillerton
correct without John Laing somewhere, even though
in the background.

John was an elderly bachelor, and lived for many
years in the village with his old mother, known in
the parish by the euphonious name of Rachie Pirie.
John must have been a sort of gardener in his young
days, and still enjoyed the monopoly of trimming
hedges, pruning trees, and of generally superintend-
ing the nurseries that supplied material for planting
the waste places of Sillerton.

I can imagine that I see John Laing before me
now—a thin, tall old man with gray hair, and cling-
ing to the stovepipe hat that, Sunday or Saturday,
he always wore.

Once he was summoned to give evidence in London
before a Committee of the House of Commons in connection with some local enterprise, and what a wealth

of story flowed from that little episode in his life! Not Stanley in his "Darkest Africa" could awaken interest in the breasts of his uncounted readers and admirers equal to the admiration that beamed in the faces of his youthful audience as Laing described his wonderful experiences on the round trip between Sillerton and London.

The modern globe-trotter would have played only second fiddle. I would not willingly touch the truthfulness of John's reports, but deep in my memory lies the conviction that the youth of Sillerton had been taught to believe, and by one who knew it too, that the choicest dish on the Royal table, and also often the only one there was "Cream porridge and cream to them."

The occupant of the other half of Laing's house was the exciseman. Now, it generally was the case that the poor exciseman was a species of pariah of society—an outcast—and that were the devil to carry him away, body and bones, there would be few old wives in Scotland who would not take up the chorus of that inimitable song of Burns—

"We wish you luck o' your prize, man !"

In Sillerton, however, no such feeling existed; the "ewie wi' the crookit horn" had long died out, and as the gauger's duties were nearly altogether confined to the operations of the distillery his intercourse with the people generally was entirely of a social character, and in consequence he became " Good-fellow-well-met " throughout that district of the country, and was more frequently and perhaps more pleasantly employed testing the good qualities of Sillerton's usquebaugh with sugar and water than in measuring the quantities that flowed into his bonded cellars, or in tramping through moss and mire to discover some venturous Scot reaping the forbidden fruits of the little still.

I remember an adventure of the exciseman that excited no little merriment in the village. The exciseman in this instance was a family man, the husband of a thrifty wife, and the proud father of at least half a dozen bairns.

It so happened that Mrs. M'Kay, in a fit of economy, suggested to her husband that their ordinary expenses would be considerably reduced were he to invest a little cash in a milch cow. The exciseman pleased, liked John Gilpin, to find that his loving spouse was possessed of a frugal mind, at once acquiesced, and as there was a "roup" at the farm of Nethermains the following week, it was decided that on that eventful day the gauger should proceed thither, and that if cows were sold for anything like feasible prices, he should become the purchaser of one, and at once bring his prize home with him.

On the day of sale the exciseman sallied forth accordingly to purchase the coveted cow. The gauger, however, no matter how competent he might be to tell the quantity and quality of a cask of whisky, felt that, in gauging the qualities of a cow, he was somewhat at sea, and so, after obtaining the opinion of two or three cronies, and treating each expert in the usual way, he himself got about half seas over; the advice or advices he had received got considerably mixed; and the result was somewhat different from what he intended, and from what his better half had desired.

Somewhere amongst the small hours the honest but fuddled gauger might have been seen leading a quadruped into the byre that had been prepared beforehand for the purchase, but as every member of his family had long ere then gone to sleep, it devolved upon Mr. M'Kay to make his cow comfortable for the night.

Somewhat later on his better half learned that the cow was awaiting her attention, and, armed with the ordinary milking pail, she proceeded to business. The result was almost fatal to Her Majesty's collector of Excise. A quadruped was in the stable, but, alas! the bovine characteristics were entirely wanting:

the obfuscated gauger had, instead of a cow, bought a horse.

The wrath of Mrs. M'Kay needed no nursing to keep it warm; it attained incandescent heat at once; and the hapless exciseman! how did he fare? Well, I would prefer not to penetrate too deeply into the secrets of any man's fireside, but this I may say, that if little milk came from the byre, there was a corresponding scarcity of the milk of human kindness everywhere about the gauger's surroundings for some time. The wags of Sillerton did not readily forget the oft-told story of the exciseman leading home by a halter his so-called cow.

CHAPTER IV.

THE DOMINIE.

And still the wonder grew
That one small head should carry all he knew.
—GOLDSMITH.

IN the tall house on the opposite side of the gate lived the Reverend Louis Alexander Daff, M. A., the parish schoolmaster. At the time I first recollect the Reverend Louis, he had retired from some of the duties of active life, and, in consequence, employed an assistant, who attended to parochial duties, while he himself enjoyed the major part of the revenue that made the parish schoolmaster an envied man. But, notwithstanding that the old dominie had not, for several years, wielded the taws in training the young ideas of Sillerton how to shoot, yet his history was peculiarly green in the memories of his contemporaries, and how often has the writer of this listened to the quaint stories of his life, and the peculiar traits of character that he had shown during an incumbency that had exceeded half a century !

Could we but hear the village worthies, as they gathered in the smithy on certain occasions, or while they crowded the merchant's shop on a Saturday evening, telling anecdotes of the old pedagogue, it would be a treat that Max O'Rell himself might long to enjoy. "Weel, he may be a very douce man noo, but, by my certie, he wisna aye that," and so out the story came, amongst many others, of how Louis preached his first sermon at Sillerton; in fact, this is a species of Scottish bull, seeing that on the occasion alluded to, when Louis certainly should have preached, Louis did not preach at all.

We may just here state, for information's sake, that the parish school was frequently the first rung of the ladder that led to the parish church, and the incumbent of the school of Sillerton, in his youth, aimed, like most other dominies, at not only "shakin' his head in a pu'pit," but at exchanging the ferula of authority that he wielded for some cosy parish church—nay, perhaps for that of Sillerton itself, which his father then occupied, and who, under ordinary circumstances, might betimes require an assistant and successor.

The old minister, therefore, was as anxious as his son that the latter should become, as soon as possible, a licensed preacher of the Gospel, and thus a fit candidate for any pastoral charge that might offer. The ordinary sessions had been taken at the Divinity Hall, the ordinary examinations had been undergone by the candidate for church patronage, and after the last, Louis Alexander was licensed by the Presbytery to preach the Gospel, the Presbytery leaving it to the licentiate to choose some church, within the bounds, where his first sermon should be preached.

Now, there was no little delicacy here. In your native parish where you had fooled with most of the young men, both in school and college days, and where, perhaps, you might have made love to a few of the prettiest maidens—and there was truly no lack of that commodity either in the village or in the parish—it was no easy matter for a participant in all these vanities to cast off at once the old slough of worldly-mindedness, trip up gayly the pulpit stairs, and become at once the monitor, nay perchance, the judge, of those who had formerly (ah! how short a time ago) joined in his folly.

But Louis Alexander had been somewhat a sly dog, and his old father had no knowledge of anything whatever that might have brought the faintest blush to the young dominie's cheek, as he entered, for the first time, his father's pulpit.

I do not exactly know what Louis' feelings were on that eventful Saturday that preceded the day when

he was, by his father's special request, to hold forth
to the parishioners of Sillerton.   Days, nay, nights
as well, had been spent in his preparations; his care-
fully-conned sermon had received its final touches;
the other parts of the service had also received due
attention, and nothing remained but that the actual
performance should be in keeping with the successful rehearsal.

Yet, notwithstanding all the preparations, Louis
Alexander was not a particularly happy man on
that eventful Saturday.

The work of the forenoon in the school engaged
his attention for some time, but as Saturday was a
half-holiday in Scotland even in those early days,
the vacant afternoon left Daff considerably too
much time to think over the trying ordeal that
awaited him in his father's pulpit the next day.
Evening came at last, and after a hurried tea, partaken of very sparingly by the embryo preacher, he
retired to his own room, leaving orders that he
should not be disturbed till breakfast time the following morning.

Gradually the shop and smithy poured forth their
respective groups of honest ploughmen that dropped
in at the village on a Saturday night to get a sock
sharpened, or perhaps to purchase an ounce or two
of good twist tobacco; maybe to get a glimpse of

some bonnie lassie that found it necessary to search around for a seemly peat wherewith to "rest" her fire for the night, for mind you those were yet scarcely the days of lucifer matches. Well, strange though it may seem, yet it invariably happened on these Saturday nights, when curfew time came, Jenny had difficulty in finding a suitable peat, and just as she was almost giving up the task in despair, Jocky chanced—mark you, "chanced"—to put in an appearance; the peat was soon found, for the youth was a good judge of these articles; the fire was speedily "rested," and Jocky was—I had almost said, soon on his way homewards.

There is no doubt this should have been the case, for the guidman and his helpmeet had long retired to the privacy of their own chamber, but somehow or other there was a difficulty in saying "good-night." No, there was no difficulty in saying "good-night," but in saying the very last "good-night." Othello knew something of this when he said, "One more, and this the last."

I believe that the Sillerton youths of that day had some idea that "good-night" was a species of adjective that had the ordinary, perhaps extraordinary, degrees of comparison. It went with them, apparently, through the positive, comparative and superlative degrees, but for some reason, that has never been fully explained, the superlative "good-night" seemed the hardest nut to crack in the lover's grammar. Certainly it was no noun, for it never seemed to be declined, and though those years have drifted far away, yet I have a most vivid recollection of the almost insurmountable difficulties that were sometimes encountered before the lips could be framed to utter honestly—that is, without equivocation or mental reservation of any kind whatever—that last—that very last—"good-night."

Sillerton was soon still as the grave. As Peter Pindar says somewhere :—

> " Now silence in the country stalk'd the dews,
>   As if she wore a flannel pair of shoes,
>   Lone list'ning, as the poets well remark,
>   To falling mill-streams and the mastiff's bark ;
>   To loves of wide-mouth'd cats, most mournful tales ;
>   To hoot of owls amid the dusky vales."

The last candle in the manse had passed beneath the extinguisher ; the last shell lamp in the village had died out, and Louis Alexander Daff, the parish schoolmaster, and the aspirant for ecclesiastical honors, is supposed to have yielded to nature's sweet restorer—sleep.

And now comes in a small additional portion of the story as it was told. Well, as to Louis, we shall see. Morning came; breakfast came also to the occupants of the manse; but Louis Alexander came not. The father was somewhat troubled at the non-appearance of his son, and a maidservant was detailed to summon the loiterer to partake of that substantial Scotch meal that in old-world homes was the meal of the day, but no Louis was there; the sheets were cold—the bird had flown.

CHAPTER V.

THE DOMINIE, CONTINUED.

Gie him strong drink until he wink,
  That's sinking in despair ;
And liquor guid to fire his bluid,
  That's press'd wi' grief and care :
There let him bouse, an' deep carouse,
  Wi' bumpers flowing o'er,
Till he forgets his loves or debts,
  An' minds his grief, no more."
                          Proverbs, xxxi., 6,7.

In the last chapter it was said that the ambitious Dominie had retired to his own room. But, alas! there was no rest there for him. Thoughts of next day's duties weighed heavily on his mind, and instead of seeking a cessation of his troubles beneath the blankets, Daff slid quietly down from his bedroom window, and sauntered leisurely along the village road.

What he intended to do or where he intended to go, as he slipped that night from his window, I am unable to say. Probably he thought that a quiet daunder would cool his blood, and predispose him to that sleep that would give him the respite of at least a few hours. At length, however, his steps somehow turned in the direction of Paradise, a species of Oriental garden that graced one of the many beautiful meadows of Sillerton, and where the chief gardener was a crony of the schoolmaster.

Daff was wont to drop in occasionally there, and generally before leaving there was produced a drop of good Scotch whisky, just for auld lang syne, in accordance with the habit and custom in those days. But, out of respect to Mr. Daff's character, we must say right here that he was universally known as a strictly temperate man, and if his conduct that Saturday night was not precisely what it should be, yet, if fall he did, he fell like better folk in Paradise, and that the weakness which on that occasion humbled him was never again, even through a long lifetime, repeated.

John Tamson, the chief gardener, on the other hand, was what the folk thereabouts called a drouthy bodie. He was given to what were known as "spates," and on those occasions, we fear, neglected his duties as the chief custodian of Paradise, and incensed accordingly his employer, Sir Archibald Gamut, the old laird. Nay, it was known that on one occasion Sir Archibald had, in great wrath, dismissed his old servant, and had, there

3

and then, ordered him to look out for another place.

The somewhat noisy sorrow of Tamson made a very evident impression on his old master, who, perhaps, in some degree relenting, demanded if he had anything to say in his own behalf that might stay the execution of the sentence that had been pronounced against him.

One peculiarity of Tamson was that while his limbs, under the influence of innumerable glasses of whisky, refused to be in any way directed by the will of their owner, in fact produced what might have been called a " locomotive strike," yet the headpiece seemed to soar above such petty weakness, and tongue and brain kept clear and cool as ever. It has been said that this gift, if it might be so called, was not confined to John Tamson, but was a peculiarity of the folks of Sillerton, although it has been said also to be common to most Scotchmen, and in fact it has been not only whispered but even printed, too, that an honest Scotch parson, after a whole evening spent in recuperating an exhausted frame, had been heard to say that he was " michtily refreshed," the refreshment indicated on this occasion being only thirteen tumblers of toddy.

Well, as to John Tamson, his limbs were sairly out of order, but with a spade in one hand, and a good grip of a yew tree, under which the laird and he were standing, he was just able to articulate a plagiarized verse of one the Psalms of David, and parodized too at that :—

> " How lovely is thy dwelling-place,
>   Sir Ar-chi-bald, to me ;
> The gravelled walks of Paradise,
>   Their like I'll never see."

When the old man reached the word " never " he became deeply moved. Had he been playing on a modern organ then, he would probably have touched the stop marked " Tremulante," but as his extemporized music was entirely vocal, it seemed as if he would never stop, and when he reached the final " see," his performance degenerated into a note that was not precisely a whine, and yet not particularly different from a genuine howl. The words and music, however, produced a softening influence upon the good laird ; his savage breast was soothed, and with a hearty roar of laughter, John Tamson's sentence was revoked, and he was relegated once more to delve about the gravelled walks of Paradise. Such was Louis Alexander Daff's host on that memorable Saturday night.

The schoolmaster's story was soon told. The old-fashioned blue bottle duly made its appearance. A few glasses of the generous, soothing liquor

found its way to the very heart of the troubled
Dominie, till, alas! the truth must be confessed,
poor Daff was overtaken, and some time amongst
the sma' hours he fell into a profound sleep. At
the time good old Daff was filling what should
have been that day his son's place in the pulpit of
Sillerton, that son was still slumbering peacefully
on the bed of John Tamson, in Paradise, for—

> " Partly wi' fear he was o'ercome,
>   And partly he was drunk,
>   That night."

A gentle whisper reached the manse, during the
afternoon, of the whereabouts of Louis Alexander,
and as the gloamin' deepened into the darkness of
a quiet Sunday summer evening, the minister's gig
deposited near the manse door the considerably
shaken-up person of the still obfuscated schoolmaster. Quietly he stole away to his own room
without obtruding his company upon his irate
father. Sleep speedily came to restore an equilibrium that had been sadly disturbed amidst the
groves of Paradise, and as the sun sent his first
rays over the parish of Sillerton, and lighted up
the heath-clad face of the distant Bennachie, the
would-be preacher awoke to commence his duties
of the week—awoke perhaps a sadder, but certainly
a wiser man.

CHAPTER VI.

THE DOMINIE MOUNTED.

So stooping down, as needs he must
　Who cannot sit upright,
He grasp'd the mane with both his hands,
　And eke with all his might.
　　　　　　　　—"*John Gilpin.*"

ONE other tale of the old Dominie that never failed to awaken the merriment of the listeners was connected with his horsemanship, which, very evidently, was not of a remarkably high order. It was just possible though that the schoolmaster had but few opportunities of studying the noble art of equestrianism. Occasionally, like some eccentric comet, the great and famous Ord appeared on the Sillerton horizon, to show off his splendid bareback riding and feats of horsemanship; yet only a few boys attempted to imitate him, and of all men in the world Louis Alexander would have been the last to follow the example.

It was also true that the eccentric Earl of Kintore occasionally rode through the village with his hunts-

men and hounds, and there were shown places where
he had made tremendous leaps in pursuit of rey-
nard, but these saltations the douce dominie would
scarcely have attempted had even Tam o' Shanter's
carlin been behind him.

Bold Buffalo Bill was then a name unknown, and
cowboys had not as yet been evolved from the quiet
Scotch herd laddie, nor, in consequence, had their
feats on Mexican plugs or bucking mustangs been
exhibited in all their glory to awaken the admiration or excite the rivalry of the British equestrian.

Without much schooling in the equinal mysteries,
therefore, Daff took kindly to a horse probably in
this way. During his more youthful days, when
juvenile ambition fills the human heart with the
intense desire of doing something that might call
down the praises of our fellow-men, he might have
pleaded guilty to the soft impeachment. Many men
at that age become imbued with martial ardor; feel
that there is that in them that might some day con-
vert them into Napoleons or Wellingtons; sigh for
a life of glory, and leaving kirk, or school, or farm
behind, join the ranks of those who seek the " bub-
ble reputation at the cannon's mouth." Well, Louis
was not one of those.

Another man is fired by tales of travel and adventure by sea and land, and the mantle of Mungo Park

falls on his shoulders, and the next thing we hear of him is he is hunting buffalo with Blackfeet Indians on the western prairies of America, or listening to an original negro melody at the sources of the Nile.

Ah! no; Louis' affections did not incline in that direction. In fact, to come to the point, his love of discovery or adventure did not spur him on far to the eastward or westward of the boundary line of the parish of Sillerton. The ambition of Daff, such as it was, was circumscribed. That ambition, though deferred for several years, was to possess a horse, and to exhibit his figure upon that quadruped's back every afternoon as far as the farm of Scrape-hard, and back again to the schoolhouse of Sillerton.

This he had done for over a year, week in and week out, wind and rain (there was no tide in Sillerton, barring a few holiday tides that were still remembered)—wind and rain we said permitting, for no man was more careful of his health than the schoolmaster of Sillerton. It was observed, however, that the dominie never once during this time had brought his equestrian exercises to a pace faster than an ordinary walk. The trot, the canter, and the gallop were utterly ignored, and had the feelings of man and beast been subjected to the operations of a mind-reader, it might have been hard to decide, to which the slow, tranquil pace was the more pleasing.

But hereby hangs a tale. Doctor Low, the village medical practitioner, had exercised his profession for some time in the district, for a doctor's field of practice in those days extended frequently over several parishes, and was bounded only by his reputation, and the ability of his nag to carry him over the long rides that he was often required to undertake. Low was, without question, a harum-scarum, a reckless horseman, and, for some reason unexplained, no admirer of the douce schoolmaster.

In Low's mind a suspicion had arisen why Daff's equestrian exercises had never exceeded the simplest movement, and overtaking him one day, just as he had turned his horse's head homeward, the mad doctor at once proceeded to test the accuracy of his suspicions. Slipping up quietly, on his nag, behind the unsuspecting Dominie, the doctor dealt Dobbin a terrible cut with his whip over the hind-quarters. The effect was electrical. Unused to such treatment, the astonished brute threw his hind heels in the air, and at a thundering gallop made for the village as if something worse than a nest of hornets was behind him.

That whip-cut also produced a very extraordinary effect upon the horseman. His seat was naturally anything but a good one, even at his usual pace, but when, without any preliminaries, the quiet, sedate walk became a terrific, thundering gallop, that seat was nowhere, or rather the seat was everywhere, now up about a foot and a half above the snorting horse, now bumped with the force of a sledge-hammer against the crupper of his saddle, and now and again changing sides, till the poor pedagogue seemed as if describing circles round a movable centre, that centre being somewhere along the spinal cord of his bounding steed.

Louis Alexander's mind, however, never lost entirely its equilibrium no matter how much that of his body was disturbed. Danger he certainly felt, but self-preservation was an inherent principle of his nature, and doing just what he was only able to do, and in this following the commendable example of the " Train-band captain of famous London Town," under somewhat similar circumstances, he leant forward upon his horse's neck, left the flowing reins to the guiding hand of chance, if to nothing better, and, with hands desperately entwined amongst the exuberant tresses of Dobbin's mane, bade fair at first to leave his tormentor behind him. But, alas! such was not to be; the village doctor was better mounted than the parish Dominie; the one nag was a fiery steed, accustomed to respond to

his rider's importunities, while poor Dobbin, even
had all other things been equal, was sadly handi-
capped, and so it came to pass that both riders entered the astonished village, not exactly neck and
neck, but Daff leading by a length.

The whole village—man, woman, and child (there
were no canines in Sillerton)—turned out to see
what the noise meant, for the triumphant medico
never missed a thwack of his whip, nor a tally-ho of
his tongue, till the sair-forfoughten Dominie found
shelter within his own gates.

There was not much law then in Sillerton ; that
was a luxury for the great ones of the earth ; and
actions for assault and battery were there utterly
unknown.

Sillerton, in fact, in this proved that history often
repeats itself, for an ancient heathen poet says in
words that, freely translated into English, would
give the stanza as under—

> " By love of right, and native justice led,
>   In straight paths of equity they tread ;
>   Nor know the bar, nor fear the judge's frown,
>   Unpractis'd in the wranglings of the gown."

The sufferer had simply to grin and bear, and the
poor schoolmaster, on account of the many bruises
. ustained by his lower limbs, was said to have worn
something resembling a kilt for ten days thereafter,

till the skin wounds were gradually and effectually healed, though some mental and even physical scars may have doubtless remained.

The village worthies delighted to tell this tale when rent-day and cracks and ale came round; and wicked Low, it was believed, never repented of what he had done, and continued, for many a year afterwards, to crack his whip and his jokes merrily as ever.

A change, however, had come over the spirit of his victim's dream; his ambition, if ambition it was, had to find vent in some other and safer channel; and the saddle and spurs, like the warrior's disused weapons, thereafter hung idly in the hall of the schoolhouse. Louis Alexander Daff never mounted steed again.

CHAPTER VII.

A DISSOLVING VIEW.

" The knights are dust ; their swords are rust ;
  Their souls are with the saints we trust."

IT appears to the author of this simple yet authentic narrative as if he had determined in his own
mind to write nothing about the folks of Sillerton
but what might excite only our risible faculties.
Now, this charge, if charge it is, we are inclined to
explain, if not indeed to deny. There might have
been, and there doubtless were, many things that
happened in the village and its surroundings in
those boyhood days of ours that were well calculated
to stir our better nature to its profoundest depths ;
there were tragedies enacted there that perhaps
sent the dagger of sorrow as straight to the heart
as when the guileless Desdemona died beneath the
hand of the loving but jealous Moor ; there were
pages of remorse written there on the stricken soul
that no pen shall ever chronicle ; tears shed that
were felt only by the cheeks over which they flowed ;

and blighted hopes there were, that death, in summer's prime, might only faintly indicate; but in life the silent lips kept their secret well, and now the humble, moss-grown tombstone tells no tales.

Some things of a saddened character certainly happened occasionally in Sillerton, and were perhaps known and felt by us also; but the tear and sigh were soon forgotten by the young, for to them the clouds return not after the rain; it was the laughter of the merry that still and ever kept ringing in our ears. And so, when much of the grave and sad has been washed away from memory by the waves of time, the merry things that happened, and the quaint and jocular stories that were told, made deeper tracks in our memories, and in consequence yet linger round us still, and rise up before us as if the wand of some mighty magician had called them all back to new-born life and action.

Well, there is nothing particularly merry before us at the present moment; there may, however, be something pleasant to contemplate, and hence enjoyable. Louis Alexander Daff—not he of youthful days nor he of robust manhood, but Daff the now superannuated schoolmaster of Sillerton, still claims a few pages of notice ere he pass by to mingle with the shadows of the past.

I can now see before me that old man, of whom I
have already said so much, weaned of the frivolities
of youth, few as they were, and descending into the
vale of years, surrounded by the respect of his
neighbors, and bearing along with him the hallowed
privileges and dignities of age.   He still enjoys his
outing, but the saddle has long given place to the
more sober social gig; Dobbin, the third in succes-
sion of that name, gray like his master, walks along in
harness, and Mrs. Daff, kindly and homely in all her
ways, is always beside her loving lord as he drives
—save the mark!—back and forth between the
eighteenth milestone and the schoolhouse of Sillerton.

Just at this point in my narrative, however,
candor compels me to say something of my own connection with the Dominie's stable arrangements, and
should the laugh be turned against me, as it certainly
has every chance of being, it must at least be borne
in mind that a barefooted callant on horseback is
very apt to ride pretty much towards the same destination which beggars under similar conditions are
said to reach.   It might help also to break my own
fall considerably to remind the reader that "he
rides siccar that never faas."

It may be as well also to mention that Daff kept
no man or boy to look after outside affairs.   A few

days of a handy laborer sufficed to plant the kail and potatoes in spring, and to house them when autumn came. In fact the servant girl was a maid of all work; looked pretty much after the nag, and faithfully bestowed upon the animal the daily allowance of oats and hay that Louis Alexander gave. Beyond, however, the feeding, Kirsty did no more, and to her the mysteries of curry-comb and brush were absolutely unknown. The truth was that had not Daff been equal to the occasion, a modern Hercules would have speedily been required to clean the Dominie's stable. But to fend off such a dilemma, Daff, cunning old rogue that he was, had succeeded in associating the brushing of Dobbin with the highest honors.

Daily for a few minutes the old man entered the schoolroom to exchange greetings with his assistant, and to inquire particularly how the Latinists were getting on. After exhorting the latter to study well and faithfully the rudiments, adding very emphatically on every occasion, "The rudiments are the very soul of the language," he detailed two of our number—Latinists, always Latinists—to brush up Dobbin for the afternoon's drive. I had often been one of the two detailed for fatigue duty, if fatigue it could be called, for the loose hairs on Dobbin were more likely to be rubbed off by our corduroy breeches

than by the regulation curry-comb. The fact was
that after a very small amount of rubbing down we
were accustomed to take the old horse out of the
stable, and with one boy on his back and another in
the rear armed with a good whip, we had lively
times of it, and doubtless refreshed our own memories of a former Dobbin's youthful gallop, with mad
Doctor Low behind him. The pig, however, goes
to the well till one day, and so with me and my
stolen rides.

My turn had now come, for my comrade was
down, and I was "up." "Boots and saddles" had
sounded, or in this case rather "Boots and no saddles," and with two or three smart cuts received
from the whip, Dobbin seemed as if he would break
the record. A shower had, however, rendered the
race-course dangerously slippery, and just as my
gallant steed turned the corner of the hen-house—
our winning post—man and horse came heavily to
the ground. No doubt a feeling of fear crossed my
mind at that supreme moment, not knowing exactly what the consequences of the tumble might
be.

Dr. Livingstone, the great African missionary and
explorer, describes his sensations under the operating teeth of an angry lion, and concludes, from personal experience, that the rat in the clutches of his

natural enemy receives a sudden shock to his nervous system that banishes both fear and suffering, and renders death almost, if not altogether, painless. This is doubtless true, but true it is also that a greater danger seems to entirely supersede a lesser one. And so in my case. In the act of falling I was sensible of the imminent danger to life and limb, but just then I caught a glimpse of the face of the thunderstruck and irate old man glaring ominously at me over the school fence.

For once in my life I played fox and lay still. The old horse, with sundry wriggles and struggles and groans, found his legs again, but I deemed it more expedient not to find mine. Instantaneously the wrath of old Daff disappeared in the stronger feeling of fear lest one of his beloved Latinists had been rendered *hors de combat*, and with kindly hands I was lifted up. My ante-mortem statement was at once taken. It was found, or at least surmised, that I was not mortally wounded. No bones were broken, so far at least as Daff's very limited anatomical knowledge might venture on an opinion. But, from the dreadful limp that at once developed, it was plain that I must be hurt somewhere. A few kindly words, however, brought back the color to my cheek, and as I expressed an ability and wish to return at once to my place among the Latinists, the

4

fears of the Dominie at once vanished, and with a little assistance I was soon in the schoolroom and at work again. I received no scolding whatever, and my comrade, who was clearly *particeps criminis,* or "airt and pairt" as we express it in Scotch, got off as well. There were sly looks as we both sat down in our places in the schoolroom to scan a few lines in Virgil, the lesson for the afternoon, and the assistant teacher, who somehow, probably from information received from Daff himself, seemed to take in the situation, could not resist the temptation of quizzing us by showing the onomatopoetic beauties of the very appropriate line, *Quadruped- ante putrem sonitu quatit ungula campum.*

Personally we did not enjoy the joke. Sore bones, and bruised muscles, and the abrasion of a few square inches of cuticle on one's person are not generally accompanied by very marked demonstrations of hilarity : and then, over and above all this, we had mental wounds as well to endure ; we knew and felt that we had lost our spurs ; curry combs and stolen gallops were no more for us ; we were reduced to the rank of infantry soldiers, and like good old Daff himself in years gone by, dismounted for another reason forever—we had had our last ride on Dobbin. It was more, however, to depict the kindlier feelings of the village Dominie that this chapter was begun than to immortalize my own exploits, may I not simply say failures? Gladly I draw a veil over this youthful escapade, and direct your eyes to a more pleasing spectacle.

Come, then, and let us take our place beside the pump that stands exactly in the middle of the tree-shaded square. The original founder of Sillerton had evidently been a mathematician, and, with a colossal pair of compasses in his hand, stuck one point down in the centre, saying, " Here is the well," and with a radius of a considerable number of yards, swung the other leg around till the circle was complete.

Round that circumference a hedge of hawthorn and beech was planted, while elm and ash trees filled the inside of the circle. One bisecting line passed through this, terminating towards one end in the door of the inn, and towards the other in the great door of the church, and affording thus on either side an easy access to the water supply for the villagers.

Round this circle ran a well-kept road, and completing it there were four rows of houses forming a rectangle rather than an exact square. The trees rose to a considerable height, and opposite to the schoolhouse a mighty elm threw out a giant arm as if to exchange courtesies with the old schoolmaster.

The steeple clock has just struck nine, but scarcely has the last stroke sounded when a window opens ; a night-capped head looks out; a kindly hand strews an abundance of crumbs upon the window-sill; a low whistle is heard, and in an instant the hoary elm is alive with birds. Roderick Dhu's whistle brought stalwart warriors innumerable from rock and tree and bracken bush, but Daff's quiet signal summons countless songsters, apparently from earth and heaven. The beautiful goldfinch is there; the more sombre chaffinch; the brilliant bullfinch; the homely but songful siskin; while a whole army at least of robin redbreasts assert their claim to human sympathy—a claim also never disputed; while a considerable colony of overbearing, pugnacious, and ubiquitous sparrows all haste into that window-sill to share in a breakfast that, Saturday and Sunday, summer and winter, is never forgotten.

Later on in the day, as the old man sits in the playground upon his easy-chair, we bring our pets to receive his praise, and a more tangible acknowledgment at the same time, and also to hear his oft-repeated admonition, " Be kind, boys, to the lower animals."

We would almost wish to stop here, but no; the whole truth must needs be told, and there are still in Sillerton men who as boys stood on that playground beside the schoolmaster, as he dispensed his praise and his pence to those who had treated his pets with kindness, and who will perhaps recollect that we did not always act on the square with the old man.

Poor Daff's eyesight had got dim, and his affection for birds and beasts was infinitely stronger than his memory. And did we not play upon these frailties? Did not the jackdaw, that, five minutes ago belonged to Jack, become in an instant the property of Gill, and that, too, by a sleight of hand that might have done credit to the "Great Wizard of the North"; and had we not frequently to hustle round to find new recruits for pay-day parade to supply the places of those who had all died in the meantime? This was very naughty on our part, but at all events, no matter our merits or demerits, Louis Alexander tried, in good faith, by rewards, to stimulate the young folks to exercise forbearance and kindliness towards the lower animals, and even if only too often his method of inculcating kindness was abused, yet still it ceased not to bear fruit.

How often have we been indebted to little incidents that happened to us in childhood for some of those tastes that thereafter grew with our growth until they influenced our whole lives, and sometimes we could scarcely tell how they originated with us ! Personally I owe much to the simple alphabet of natural history that the old teacher taught me on the playground of Sillerton.

On the playgreen of Sillerton there was little taught of the natural history of science, but there was much of that natural history with which the kindlier feelings of the heart have to do. We certainly learned but little there of the great classes into which the animal kingdom was divided ; orders, families, genera, species, and varieties were not household words with the kindly schoolmaster, but if watching a ruby-throated humming bird sipping its nectar and drawing its other supplies from the storehouse of a flower, or listening to the newly-arrived Canadian rossignol pouring forth its sweet song, long ere the March winds had ceased to blow —if these are pleasures that I have been privileged to enjoy, how much of that enjoyment owed its very existence to the suggestive example of the kind Dominie; and the oft-repeated maxim, spoken on the schoolgreen of Sillerton, so many long years ago, still whispers in my ear, even amidst the solitudes of the primeval forest, "Boys, be kind to the lower animals." We owe this tribute, and we pay it willingly, to the memory of the kind old man.

The end came calmly as the quiet of a summer gloaming. The birds, as their wont was, flocked to the unopened window, but no breakfast awaited them that morning; the hands that had long dispensed the crumbs to those that neither sow nor reap were folded in rest; the heart that had so often sent forth its warm sympathies to the lower formations of the Creator's hand was cold and still; there was indeed a vacancy not only in the school of Sillerton, but in its village square as well; the fluttering and twittering of the little winged orphans around the unopened schoolhouse window, and the absence of the well-known white nightcap, were the first intimation to the villagers that their kindly neighbor would never again feed and clothe the poor, nor scatter crumbs to the little songsters that were still awaiting him at the draped window; and soon all that was mortal of the Rev. Louis Alexander Daff was laid to rest beside his kindred dust in the old churchyard.

After the funeral, a few friends gathered in the schoolhouse, as was the custom, to hear the will read. Daff had been a careful man, and left behind him a considerable amount of worldly wealth. Due provision was therefore made for the sorrowing widow; and, true to his character, amongst the legacies there was a weekly allowance set apart for

Dobbin, and an annual dole set aside also for the board of a favorite cock, these sums to be paid during the natural term of their lives.

Strange to say, twenty years thereafter old Dobbin was still to be seen on the braes of Fetternear, and that identical cock was still crowing then, as if, like the eagles, he had renewed his age.

Did a superabundance of kindly care keep the legatees in life? Did the caretaker of these two happy orphans discover and administer to his wards some elixir of life that enabled them to enjoy the bounty of their departed master long after the period usually allotted to the equine or the gallinaceous animals; or was it possible, as some miserable misanthropes hinted, that old Dobbin and his ancient comrade had long ago ceased to neigh and crow, but that fit representatives had been found to enjoy that bounty that the village schoolmaster bestowed upon at least two of the lower animals in his last will and testament?

With the old squire we might say, "Much might be said on both sides."

> " He prayeth best who loveth best
>   All things both great and small ;
> For the dear God who loveth us,
>   He made and loveth all."

CHAPTER VIII.

THE STICKIT LAWYER.

The poor inhabitant below
Was quick to learn and wise to know,
And keenly felt the friendly glow
    And softer flame ;
But thoughtless follies laid him low,
    And stain'd his name.
               The Bard's Epitaph.

WE have looked into the last will and testament of Louis Alexander Daff, whose tombstone still adorns the quiet churchyard of Sillerton ; but ere "we draw the curtain down," we would fain point out one other scene in this connection, so to speak, and touch, it may be but lightly, upon the other members of the Daff family. There is little to be said of them, but yet that little seems necessary to fill up and render complete, as it were, the background. Two maiden sisters and a ne'er-do-weel brother, Sandy, complete the group.

Sandy was certainly an M. A. of Aberdeen, as we shall see or hear, it may be, by and by, but he attained the position of only a stickit lawyer, and

reached no higher. Some small provision had been
made for the two old maids, and with assiduous
care they were able to keep a roof over their heads
in a neighboring parish; the said roof also, though
of heather, sheltered as well poor spendthrift Sandy.

Their brother the schoolmaster died in the spring,
and as the appointment of a successor would not
take place for some little time, a considerate friend,
the very reference to whom brings a tear to my eye,
suggested that it would be a work of charity to put
in a crop in the dead man's garden for the benefit of
the living members of the family. This was quietly
accomplished. The left hand, in this case, did not
know what the right hand had done. Potatoes had
been planted in the old monks' garden; a reasonable
amount of labor had been bestowed upon them, and
when the autumn came the increase seemed to have
become at least thirty-fold.

I was then a stripling attending a neighboring
school, and passing every day the door of the Daff
family. It was now necessary to inform them what
had been done, and I had received a suitable message,
though it might have been altered in my mind and
memory as I hurried on to school. I knocked at the
humble door as directed, and instantly two thin,
worn, ancient maidens stood before me, and rather
curtly demanded my business.

Somewhat confused, I blurted out—"The taties are ready for houkin' in the schoolyard o' Sillerton, and your brither Sandy better gae up and look after them." Ye gods! what a scraich greeted me. "Sandy! What Sandy dae ye mean? Sandy! Sandy! Sandy!" rising in the inflection till the last "Sandy" reached a note that I have never since heard, even through the trained lips of a prima-donna. "Ye aiblins mean Maister Alexander Daff, our brither. He is nae Sandy, but a Maister o' Airts of Aberdeen, for weel-a-wat our father paid good siller for the honor—Sandy, did ye say?" But I had heard and seen enough; a species of terror now added wings to my feet, and I heard no more. The Master of Arts, however, Sandy or no Sandy, duly put in an appearance, and the potatoes that grew in the school-house garden of Sillerton were boiled by the maiden sisters of the Master of Arts.

I remember well one of Sandy's tricks. Fond of a little tobacco was he, but seldom was he able to indulge in that luxury. Fortune, however, on one occasion at least, deigned to favor him. A sad in-flux of caterpillars came, the berry bushes were in imminent danger, and tobacco smoke alone could put to flight the enemy. Poor Sandy for once in his life was happy. The ill wind blew him good on this occasion. His sisters purchased a few ounces of twist; a pipe was procured, no matter where, and I had several times the pleasure of seeing the Master of Arts smoking away contentedly the pests that threatened to bring ruin upon his sisters' gooseberries.

A whole week was spent in the conscientious performance of duty, and had the sisters' purse held out, Sandy Daff would have smoked on, without one grumble at the trouble it cost him, till the berries were falling from the bushes, or to latter Lammas for aught I know.

One incident more I shall relate to fill up the background I have attempted to paint, and we shall then finish with the Daff family.

Sandy was fond of tobacco, but Sandy was also fond of whisky. Hence those tears! hence the stickit lawyer! hence a misspent life, and smoking vile tobacco beneath a gooseberry bush, when instead, arrayed in silken gown, he should have been reaping a golden harvest at the bar. But such, alas! was not for Sandy. Occasionally he reached Sillerton on Saturday evening, but for what purpose it were hard to say. Long habit, may have made the journey chronic, if journeys ever become so, but the chance of a drop of the barley bree was inducement enough to him to walk a few miles on the pleasures of hope. One Saturday evening he had, for probably good cause, been turned out of the village shop. Sandy bent to the inevitable, but he recollected and winced under the insult. In those primitive days a monthly market was held in the town of Inverurie, and there congregated business men from every surrounding district. Sandy was waiting and watching for his revenge.

Down, next market day, came slowly about a dozen riders from Sillerton. They must needs pass very close to Daff's humble dwelling. As they approached, the Master of Arts rushed forward to meet them, stood on the highway, and most obsequiously lifted his hat to the shopkeeper, who was one of the party, and who, little more then a week before, had turned him out of his store.

Pleased by Sandy's attention, Baggs, who was a vain man, drew up his nag, and addressed his respectful friend. This was just what and all that Sandy wanted. Emitting a series of sounds that were admirably adapted to express his contempt, he turned away hastily on his heel, muttering loud enough to be heard by all the party—" Excuse me, sir; I mistook you for a gentleman." If the scowl that came from one, and the roar of laughter that rose from all the rest were worth anything, Sandy had won a sweet revenge.

Not very long after, that small building was tenantless—the two sisters had passed away—and the schoolmaster's brother, Sandy Daff, the Aberdeen Master of Arts, soon followed. In him death gleaned the last sheaf of the Daff family. Alas! poor Yorick!

CHAPTER IX.

DOCTOR LOW'S WATCH LOST AND FOUND.

Ye ken Jock Hornbook i' the clachan,
Deil mak' his king's-hood in a spleuchan ;
He's grown sae weel acquaint wi' Buchan
    An' ither chaps,
The weans had oot their fingers laughin',
    An' pouk my hips.

                    BURNS.

DOCTOR Low had in youthful, palmy days accelerated the movements of young Dobbin and his canny
master from Nethermains to the village of Sillerton.
But this was many years before I knew Sillerton, and
it was only the old stories that I heard. But I also
knew Low.

In a small " fell " biggin', in somewhat advanced
age, and alone, lived the old doctor. But Low's
occupation was gone. The places that knew him
once now knew him no more. New kings had risen
that knew not Joseph. Young science had made
strides that left the old practitioner behind. Like the
old three-deckers whose last shot had been fired, and
which now, giving place to the ironclads of a recent

day, lay stranded, useless hulks upon the shore, so
a younger and better educated class of medicals had
come in to place their predecessors high and dry
upon the shelf; and the old practitioners, if they had
failed to provide something for a rainy day, now
sank into abject poverty, or depended upon the
charity of one or two who enabled them to live without knowing that they were actual paupers. Such,
alas! was poor old Low.

Times had gone hard with the old man. Ah!
could he have lived upon the stories about himself
that the writer of this has listened to, he would have
died of obesity. And such stories, too! Our grand-
fathers, and grandmothers also, had a plain way of
talking, and told tales in the drawing-room that
could not now be whispered in the kitchen, for the
modern cook would blush at the recital and the
pretty housemaid would play bopeep through her
fingers, and declare that old fellows like Low were
very naughty boys indeed.

Well, I may not, and shall not, tell all the funny
things that I have heard about the old doctor; but
one story at least may be told, and no one need
blush at its recital. Christmas and New Year were
drawing near, and all the parish was bent on enjoyment. But there was one exception. In that turf-
built cottage an old man is sitting on his so-called

easy-chair; the little shell lamp that burns beside him helps the December day to look longer than it really is; and the bright peat fire sheds a ruddy glow (that would have charmed the eye of a Rembrandt,) over the old doctor's face, as my father and I, after a quiet knock upon the door, lift the latch and " step ben " as the cheery welcome strikes our ears.

With kindly tact the truth is elicited that funds had never been at so low an ebb before; the Yule and New Year that promised so much pleasure to almost all, had no welcome tidings for poor, poverty-stricken Low; and as he dwelt fondly upon the rude yet hearty experiences of merrymakings now long gone by, and in which he himself played no unimportant part, a slight quaver came softly from his lips, and one big tear of regret rolled down his wrinkled cheek. The kindly visitor, however, had not come there that evening to add to the old man's sorrows, but to take some of them away if possible, and in a quiet and sympathetic way it was suggested that the doctor's gold watch should be shot for on Old Christmas Day by the sporting youths of Sillerton.

The passing of the watch into other hands would have occasioned its present possessor no inconvenience whatever. It was now many years since the old timekeeper had in fact struck work. Its owner

5

firmly believed that the motion connected with exercise on horseback was necessary to bring out all its sterling qualities, and that its silence now was caused simply because its wearer no longer patronized the gallop, but had descended to the more sober pace of "Shank's mare." Be that, however, as it may, it was then and there agreed to, that the gold watch should be shot for at Mains of Pitfuffie on old Christmas day; that subscription lists should be at once opened; and that the successful shot should wear the gold watch. *Qui meruit palmam ferat,* was the motto of our Sillerton Wapinschaw. Steadily went on the canvass during the days that intervened between that December evening and the day of the great shooting match.

There was no limit to the number of subscribers; the ancient timepiece possessed a value that half-crowns scarcely indicated; and when the youth of Sillerton stood to their guns on the heights of Pitfuffie on that bleak January morning (remember it was old style that we kept then) it was found that the old watch had realized for its owner nearly forty pounds sterling, no small sum amongst that quiet and simple people, and a perfect godsend to the impecunious old man. The cash had all been deposited in the hands of the umpire, the rules and regulations had been duly read, and the firing briskly began.

Old Christmas was certainly a legal holiday in Sillerton, though there were neither bank clerks nor Government officials there to enjoy their privileges, and it devolved upon the schoolboys alone, with a few dozen ploughmen and hobbledehoys of the parish, to demonstrate that this was a day to be devoted fully and freely to social liberty and enjoyment. Steadily from morn to night the guns blazed away, and the roll of subscribing marksmen was not completed until the shades of evening began to creep across the scarred brows of Bennachie. No shot had gained a bull's eye, though there were a score at least of ties that had almost grazed the black ball that marked the centre. These ties were about to be shot off, when the remark was made that my father, who had collected nearly nine-tenths, of the whole amount, and who was as well a liberal subscriber, was not on the ground, and had not claimed a shot.

It was then and there carried by acclamation that a shot should be fired on his behalf, his proxy being the exciseman, who was unquestionably the best shot in the parish. It was agreed, at the same time, that the ties should be fired off after the gauger's shot. A few moments of intense suspense came; the exciseman during that time looked as if carved out of Millstonehill granite; a puff of blue smoke at last came from the old musket, while every breath was hushed, and every eye strained to catch a glimpse of the now battered target. The marker quietly and deliberately performed his duty, and then lei-surely faced the expectant crowd. At last the signal came—a bull's eye! One shout rose over the field; no ties had to be shot off; the watch, the gold watch of the old doctor, had been waged and won, and in less time than it takes to tell it, I was hurrying homeward with that gold watch nestling in my breast pocket, while the temporary custodian of the same felt as proud and happy as if he had won and worn the Victoria Cross.

What were the thoughts that passed through my mind as I sped homewards that evening, I can scarcely tell. Probably I thought that as my father required but one watch, I was likely to become the happy owner of the gold one, but if not of that coveted prize, yet I felt that one of the watches must fall to my lot, assuredly under any circumstances.

No sooner had my father arrived than I hastened to exhibit to him the trophy that he had won. He assured me that there was some mistake, as he had claimed no shot. I then recounted the occurrences of the day, and the firing of the shot that made the bull's eye. I shall never forget the look of sadness that stole over his features as I told my story. Probably he felt in his own mind that I was too young to take it upon myself to refuse the prize, but I know I felt supremely happy at that moment that I had expressed no craving for the ownership of the doctor's watch, and I believe he never once suspected the nature of my feelings. " Go," said he, " at once to Dr. Low ; give him again his watch with my compliments and say that I hope he may be long spared to wear it." Then in a low voice he added—" I would not that that old man should fall asleep this night without his watch, no, not for all the gold watches that were ever made."

As I placed the prize half an hour later in the old doctor's hand, with my father's compliments and wishes, I heard no word of thanks spoken, but a silent tear stole down the furrowed cheek. I had seen a tear there once before ; a tear of regret as he looked backward to a prosperous and merry past that could never return, and as he felt and feared that only a gloomy future was in store for him. The tear that came now was the handmaid of a grateful heart, and whispered a message of deepest thanks that no language could have expressed so well. I returned home glad that I no longer wore a watch. Did my father feel that night that it was more blessed to give than to receive ?

CHAPTER X.

HOW MARY MITCHELSON DISHED HER HUSBAND'S BROSE.

> " She has an ee, she has but ane,
> The cat has twa the very color,
> Sic a wife as Willie had ! "

TALL, wall-sided, speaking a dialect neither Scotch nor English, but made up of both, and wearing a green patch over one eye—such was the subject of this sketch. This rude outline might have been drawn a year or two before old Dobbin became an orphan, and while John Forres, a young teacher from a peculiarly quiet and secluded parish of Aberdeenshire, was assistant to the old schoolmaster. I shall have occasion to touch lightly upon the young dominie by and by.

Mary Mitchelson I called her, but probably I should have designated her Mrs. George Brodie. It was the custom, however, in Sillerton, and probably elsewhere, for some married ladies to retain their maiden names, just as ladies, in these modern days, celebrated in literature or art, or by rank or riches, often retain the name under which they won their spurs, if I may be allowed to use the expression with reference to the fair sex. It seems to me indeed that this was more commonly the usage, perhaps I should have said universally the usage, when the gray mare was the better horse.

Well, Mary Mitchelson was a woman of pronounced character, and affected a style of language and genteel manners that seemed considerably above her social position as a Sillertonian. Poor, simple, homely Geordie Brodie was only a sawyer, and before saw-mills were common in Sillerton earned his living by converting the Scotch firs that covered nine-tenths of the parish into boards and scantling.

The labors of a sawyer were necessarily severe, and as long distances had frequently to be traversed between the home of the laborer and his workshop, it was no wonder that Geordie Brodie often returned home weary, ay, weary and hungry as well. This was just as it should be under ordinary circumstances; and when there was the wherewithal to satisfy the cravings of hunger, the fact itself should have suggested a feeling of gratitude, for our national bard puts it thus—

> " Some hae meat and canna eat,
>   And some wad eat that want it ;
> But we hae meat and we can eat,
>   And sae the Lord be thankit."

I have said that the sawyer should have been grateful for the feeling of hunger under ordinary circumstances, but there was something more than ordinary in this case. Geordie Brodie and Mary Mitchelson were not precisely at one with regard to the quantity of eatables that should satisfy the gnawing appetite of a healthy, hungry man. Mary, in fact, must have been first cousin to Mrs. Squeers, of Do-the-boys Hall, though she did not adopt the same tactics in turning the edge of the appetite.

And so it happened that the sawyer frequently, nay, invariably, complained of receiving short commons on his nightly return from his arduous labors. Philosophers had long ago discovered that "Nature abhorred a vacuum," but it needed no philosopher to discover that when a vacuum existed in a man's stomach, the owner of said stomach was ill at ease with himself and the world at large. Mary ignored this fact, and day after day, and week after week, continued to dole out to Geordie a measure of brose to his supper that lacked at least a third of the quantity that he considered should fall to his lot. Complaints, grumblings, and recriminations in consequence passed between the pair, until one evening matters came to a climax, and Geordie Brodie absolutely refused to even taste his usual allowance.

Mary, instead of yielding that obedience that she had doubtless once promised, bitterly resented her husband's "evil temper," as she was pleased to call it, and brooded in silence over her own fancied wrongs. During the following day the same feeling absorbed her thoughts, until near the time when preparation had to be made for Geordie's return.

Suddenly a happy thought seemed to strike Mrs. Brodie, and a smile of satisfaction flitted across her saturnine, pinched features. Eureka (I have found it), Mary might have exclaimed, had she known Greek, but, Greek or no Greek, she had found a happy solution to the problem that she had been so long pondering in her mind. To think, with Mary, was to act. She at once rose from her seat beside the fire that she had been stirring in anticipation of preparing her husband's evening meal, and hastened to the byre, that was only a few dozen of yards from the house. There, providing herself with the wooden trough in which the cow was usually supplied with her allowance of boiled turnips and chaff, Mary was soon again in her own kitchen. The trough was duly placed on the table where Geordie Brodie's cap of brose usually stood; a large quantity of oatmeal, butter, and boiling water were stirred together in the lordly dish, and with a grim smile of satisfaction, Mary awaited the dénouement.

She had not long to wait. Brodie almost immediately entered the little apartment that served the
double purpose of kitchen and dining-room, and
hungry and tired, as usual, his eye naturally turned
to the table. A sarcastic jibe from his better-half
might have accelerated his scrutinizing glance. Be
that, however, as it may, the hungry sawyer took
in the whole situation at once. And then, what a
storm arose! Little did the wife anticipate the
furious rage that, in one moment, converted the
quiet and douce Geordie Brodie into a raving maniac.
But so it was.

What then and there took place was never known.
Geordie Brodie went next morning to his daily toil
as usual. Young Geordie—for they had one son—
looked after such matters as required some attention outside, and only after a long month's seclusion
did Mary Mitchelson appear in the Sillerton Square.
But an altered woman was she. Her stiff and un-
shapely form seemed even more acute-angled than
before; the sarcastic smile was perceptibly intensified, and to crown all there was a green patch over
one of her eyes, that was never removed during the
many years that she thereafter lived in Sillerton.
Poor Mary had few friends, and did little to con-
ciliate the few who might have been friendly to her.
Her bite was ever readier than her smile, and scath-

ing sarcasm came more freely and naturally from her lips than commendation and praise. Sarcasm, indeed, with Mary Mitchelson was always upon a hair-trigger.

Once more we venture to fill up a background.

The son, Geordie junior, was a pupil in the parish school, at this time taught by the assistant of Louis Alexander. One day during the recital of the fore-noon lessons, the door suddenly opened, the face of Mary Mitchelson appeared, and a shrill and some-what angry voice demanded—"George! where did you put the jocktaleg before you went to school?" The question was put in words that stood out singly, as it were, and which were scarcely in the style commonly used in Sillerton. Very different were the accent and tone that came from Geordie, "In the greep ahint the coo, mither."

The effect was irresistible. Even the smallest Scotch heads took it in. One roar of laughter rose from all present, which was also participated in by the youthful assistant. Mary, however, quailed not under the ridicule that her visit and question had evoked, but, ignoring all the others, she fixed her one eye upon the poor but guilty dominie, and speak-ing slowly, as if desiring that every word she uttered should be a species of dagger-thrust, she annihilated him with the scathing remark. "What—could—

you—expect—out—of—Leochel ? " Leochel, I may
explain, was the native parish of the teacher.   The
door banged loudly and Mary Mitchelson was gone.
Her remark, however, remained behind, and became
a byword in the parish of Sillerton, and I doubt
not, were I fortunate enough to ever revisit those
scenes of my boyhood, I should still hear, many a
time, a free and Scotch translation of the Jewish
proverb, "Can any good thing come out of Naz-
areth."

CHAPTER XI.

THE QUEEN'S SCOTCH AS SPOKEN IN SILLERTON.

But he, I ween, was of the north countrie.
BEATTIE'S " Minstrel."

IT was stated in the foregoing chapter that Mary
Mitchelson spoke a dialect somewhat different from
that used in Sillerton. At the same time it may be
explained, that, for causes to be given, the Scotch
of the Sillertonians was not precisely identical with
that spoken in other parishes of the Garioch, and
especially in places lying to the west and north of
the parish.

It is curious sometimes to note the effects produced even by a range of hills surrounding a small
community, and shutting it out, so to speak, from
other communities; effects that influence, in no
small degree, language, character, both mental and
physical, and last, but not least, religion itself. I
recollect well, in boyhood's days, when spending my
holiday among the hills that lie between the Don
and Spey, I more than once came upon a commu-

nity of Roman Catholics living snugly in some sheltered valley that had remained uninfluenced by the great Reformation that had swept over Scotland, but which had passed them by, simply on account of the gigantic bulwark of rocks and hills that rendered communication with the people living within this barrier very difficult, if not well-nigh impossible.

I remember meeting on the Gaudie side of Bennachie, two members of the Royal Academy of Painters, one of whom, the celebrated so-called "Philip of Spain," was searching closely for types of genuine Scottish faces, with which to fill up a historical scene he was painting. I sent him to such a spot as I have just described, the Cabrach, and years afterwards he assured me that he had found there exactly what he wanted. As to the influence of such a locality on language there can be no doubt whatever, and hence the Grampian range, that sheltered Sillerton from the west and north, rendered Sillerton's speech somewhat different from that spoken beyond the dividing line.

There were other causes as well to influence our speech. Sillerton was, in one respect, somewhat ambitious, and amongst the farmers who cultivated its fair meadows and sunny slopes there were several who had enjoyed the privilege of a college education. I do not mean to say that these men had given themselves the trouble of working for a degree in Arts, but four years at the University had made them at least fair scholars, while four years' intercourse with youths drawn from all parts of Scotland served, in no small measure, to influence their Doric Scotch, and through them to influence others with whom they were daily associated. The degrees were more in the way of professional men; and ministers, schoolmasters, and medicals (we seemed to educate no lawyers in Sillerton) deemed it at least advisable to go in for the degree of M. A.

From this it is evident that the Queen's Scotch was somewhat different among the upper ten of Sillerton society, for we were strictly conservative in those days, and when invited to a dance, dinner, or picnic, could always tell precisely who the individuals were, they at least of the parish, who would receive and accept invitations. All this had its influence beyond the immediate circle, like the stone cast into a still pond, that not only makes a splurge in the very spot where it falls, but sends countless ripples away on every side to the very shore. In fact, one can scarcely conceive how easily and readily language is affected by the circumstances that surround us, and I remember well the remark of a pawky farmer of Sillerton in corroboration of this assertion on our part. A neighbor remarked that his "orra" man spoke in a style quite different from that used by the other servants. "Oh, aye," said the carl, "I ance sent Jock on some business to the Lothians; he was awa a hale fortnicht, and he has spoken pure English ever Since syne."

There was also another factor at work which in due course affected the Queen's Scotch as spoken in Sillerton. Not many years before the commencement of my school-days, a good deal of Scotch was spoken by our schoolmasters, and it was no uncommon circumstance to hear a commentary on a chapter of the Bible conducted from the pulpit in genuine Scotch.

This was not the case with the Rev. Robert Fordyce, for with him both bearing and language were dignity personified; but slightly farther north the old Scotch still held its sway, and an esteemed class-fellow of mine told me that he heard a noted divine, not many miles from Aberlour, use the following "grace before supper" on one occasion— "For what I and the ither three lads are aboot to receive, Lord, mak' us a' truly thankfu'. Amen."

In this case, however, we must bear in mind that there was no doubt whatever about what language the speaker intended to use, and the Rev. Mr. Wilson, of Aberlour, spoke Scotch because he liked to speak it, and because probably he found himself more at home in it than were he using the Queen's English.   But in the case of educated men who knew English well, who could spell it correctly, and, were perfectly conversant with its grammar and idioms, we are well aware that they were frequently not acquainted with the proper vowel sounds. This fact is pointed out in the life of the author of "Tullochgorum."   In one of Skinner's pieces, which is written in the purest English, the rhyme shows this defect.   The piece we refer to is "John of Badenyon," and it is at least interesting to note how frequently the long sound of "o" is made to ryhme to the last syllable of the name of the hero, which is unquestionably short.   Of course it might be pleaded that there are certain "allowable rhymes," and that the greatest English poets have availed themselves of the privilege when necessary.

In Pope we find the following lines—

> Thus Pegasus, a nearer way to take,
> May boldly deviate from the common track ;

and in Dryden we have the following :—

> The sun his annual course obliquely made.
> Good days contracted and enlarg'd the bad.

We might indeed quote such examples by the

6

hundred. This was undoubtedly a species of poetical
license, but among my own personal clerical friends
there were a half-dozen at least, who, in certain
vowel sounds, and especially when in the pulpit,
used liberties with the Queen's English positively
startling, and it always appeared a puzzle to me
how such pronunciation could have been acquired.
But such it was.

Doubtless, the introduction of railways, and a
freer intercourse between the natives on both sides
of the Tweed have done much during the last half-
century to enable even the more highly-educated
Scot to distinguish correctly between the different
sounds of the same vowel, and we doubt not, that
the next northern bard who tries his hand at a new
version of "John o' Badenyon" will steer clear,
without difficulty, of those solecisms that were ere-
while committed by the genial pastor of Linshart.

I knew intimately a very excellent divine on
Donside; a man distinguished for his learning;
valued and honored in Church courts; eloquent
either on the platform or in the pulpit; and above
all one of the most genial of men, and yet as to his
pronunciation of the Queen's English he was a veritable barbarian. The witty editor of an Aberdeen
weekly remarked, that it was a pity that the learned
and popular minister of T—— had, in his youth, got

a spurious edition of Walker's pronouncing dictionary.

But, after all, are these things to be considered strange in the case of Scotchmen, when we find Englishmen themselves sometimes, nay oftentimes, anything but correct in the pronunciation of their own language?

I have heard in an English Cathedral from the lips of a graduate of an English University, and from one, too, enjoying those marks of distinction after his name that stamp men eminent for scholarship—I have heard, I say, false pronunciation of English that was perfectly startling. Need we wonder then when we hear an educated Scotchman calling a Presbyterian Synod "this reverend coort," or employing equally eccentric modes of speech that should have been eliminated, if not in the nursery, then in the parish school?

I may remark here, that the inspectorship of schools also, in connection with bequests that applied to our parochial system, made it imperative that a sound English education should be given in our schools, and while the classics and mathematics scarcely jarred with the pure Doric of the Garioch, yet with the teaching of English it was quite different.

It was indeed difficult to find teachers in those

days who had anything like a correct idea of the different vowel sounds, and how could they, under the circumstances? Many of our teachers held that English grammar was unnecessary where the Latin grammar had to be taught, and hence, while spelling and some other things were correct enough, yet the pronunciation was sadly defective.

Here, however, is a case in point. The inspector of the Dick Bequest was examining a school not far from the shady side of Bennachie, and took occasion to correct a class for their inattention to the different sounds of the vowel " u," the word " bull " having occurred in the lesson, and pointing out in the dictionary key, how the vowel should be sounded in different words. The dominie could not stand this, but interrupted the proceedings with the remark, " Na, na, sir; it's bull, full, pull," pronouncing the three words in the broadest Doric, Scotch, " an' the loons are richt."

This may be an exceptional case, but doubtless its existence in a greater or less extent brought it about, that when a vacancy occurred in Sillerton, the place was filled by young men who had enjoyed a town training in addition to the usual classical education. This was truly the piece of leaven that leavened the lump.

Old Louis Alexander Daff indoctrinated his pupils

with as pure Latinity as we got from the more modern teachers, but the latter taught us English Grammar, and gave us such a pronunciation of English as would enable us to become tutors in any of our more ambitious Scotch families, or even successful teachers beyond the border in English schools.

Gentle reader, bear in mind that it is not here pretended that the youths of Sillerton succeeded in acquiring an English accent. No, no; not often do we find Scotchmen who do this, and while we occasionally meet our countrymen who were perhaps educated in England, and who had been long strangers to the land of the heather, speaking a language that would scarcely indicate their nationality, yet when we enter into familiar conversation with them, there generally slips out a word or phrase that betrays its northern origin. It is not universally the case that the accent remains, but it is very frequently so, and in proof I may mention an incident that happened in my own experience. Dining at a mess table, where I had the honor of performing the duties of regimental chaplain, an English lady who sat next to me said, " How is it that Scotchmen so often retain their Scotch accent, even after many years' absence from Scotland ? I have often asked the question, but I confess that I have never received a satisfactory answer." I replied that I felt satisfied that it would be unnecessary for her to ask the same question again, as I could give a conclusive answer. "How is it then?" she inquired. Raising my head, and looking as dignified as possible. I replied, "We are proud of our accent."

"Ah! I just thought as much."

There was a slight lull in the conversation, and I very quietly threw in the additional information. "But, madam, there is another reason, for were we to try to get rid of our accent I do believe that we would find it impossible." It is needless to say that I brought down the house and that my fair questioner laughingly remarked, "I am quite satisfied now."

I shall close this chapter with showing the care that our pedagogues took not only in teaching what they held to be pure English, but in getting their pupils to read with an eye to punctuation as well, without which the sense of the passage might have escaped them altogether. A neighboring teacher fell upon the unique plan of getting his pupils to pronounce the word "tick" whenever a comma occurred in a sentence; a semi-colon and colon received two "ticks," while the full stop elicited three "ticks." This was to be practised, however, for a short time only, and as the school examination approached, the "ticks" were duly dropped, and "dummy ticks," so to speak, were used instead. The great day at last came, and the Bible-class was paraded for duty. Unfortunately the dux had been absent for a few days, and had not been made aware of the new order for abolishing the " ticks."

The chapter for the day was duly pointed out, and the dux, evidently in his nervousness, skipping several important parts of the passage, yet, in a clear and distinct voice, astonished the listening divines with a new rendering of the Scripture lesson:— " And the Lord said unto Moses, tick, say unto the children of Israel, tick, tick; and Moses said unto the children of Israel, tick, tick, tick."

And lastly, as some of our preachers were wont to say, even after the conclusion, I shall instance the case of Willie Nuckel, so called, a crofter in the village, who nearly lost his croft by inattention to the due punctuation of his speech, if I may so designate the blunder. Nuckel evidently had never been duly drilled in school days in the proper use of the " ticks," and in consequence nearly came to grief. Nuckel was the owner of a horse called Diamond, why so called I am now unable to say—probably for some excellent qualities that the animal possessed. In those days few pedestrians were allowed to pass through the Home Park, which separated the laird's residence from the village of Sillerton, and to be seen there with a horse and cart, or in fact with any vehicle whatever, would have been considered a species of sacrilege.

Nuckel, however, had received orders from the proper quarter, and early one morning was met by the laird while carting a load of fallen branches from the said park to the village. The somewhat irate proprietor demanded of Nuckel, and not in very pleasant tones, why and what he was carting there.

Nuckel was decidedly in a hurry, and was little inclined to parley with any one, the only words heard by the squire being, "Sticks for the forester ye brute—Diamond, get up."

Poor Nuckel was served with the usual notice to leave his croft and cottage at next Martinmas, the laird having imagined that the word "brute" was applied to himself personally. A due explanation stayed the sentence, and Nuckel sleeps in Sillerton churchyard. The obnoxious epithet, after all, was really not intended for the laird, but for the horse: but still the proper application of the "tick" in the right place, would have in this case saved days and weeks, nay, months, of misery.

CHAPTER XII.

JEAN BARDEN'S MILK FOR BABES.

Though the " Brownie o' Blednoch " lang be gane,
The mark o' his feet's left on mony a stane ;
An' mony a wife an' mony a wean
      Tell the feats of Aiken-drum.

E'en now, light loons that jibe an' sneer
At spiritual guests an' a' sic gear,
At the Glashnoch mill hae swat wi' fear,
      An' looked roun' for Aiken-drum.

And guidly folks hae gotten a fright,
When the moon was set, and the stars gied nae light,
At the roaring linn in the howe o' the night,
      Wi' sughs like Aiken-drum.
             The Brownie o' Blednoch.

I often wonder if those who were most zealous in indoctrinating our young minds with all the superstitions of those days ever reflected on the great wrong they were doing. I wonder if they ever thought that it would take, in some cases, the effort of years to root out the weeds that they were then so anxious to sow ; nay, that in some cases so deeply would these weeds penetrate into the mind, that they would grow with our growth, and blossom as freely in old age, as when we clung to our mother's apron strings.

It is said that noted travellers who have spent years amongst savage tribes, even when they return to civilization, dread to hear a footstep behind them, and peer cautiously into a room before they enter it. And men I have personally known, who had borne themselves bravely through many a hard-fought and bloody field, yet when the shadows of night came down, would not have gone alone a hundred yards in the dark, no matter what the bribe might be that sought to tempt them. And all this, at least in the latter case, very probably originated in the habit, doubtless long established, of telling stories of a blood-curdling character to the young.

Jean Barden was pre-eminently the story-teller of Sillerton. It was true that the meal-miller could spin a wonderful yarn about water-kelpies and their strange doings, and how the miller word, when properly and artistically handled, could instantaneously arrest a water-wheel in full career and perform sundry other wonderful things—all of which tales were greedily swallowed by many of the miller's audience, for audience he often had when the first oats of the season began to arrive at Damhead. But the burly miller could not hold a

candle to Jean, who, both in yield and variety, dis-
tanced every competitor.

The fact is, that at this distant date, it would be
difficult to specify exactly the points possessed by
Jean that enabled her to outstrip all other rivals.
It is possible that one point was the variety of
beings of supernatural origin that filled her reper-
toire.

The miller had only two strings to his bow—the
miller word and the water-kelpie; the blacksmith,
during the intervals that occurred between the
hammering of the iron and the reheating of it
again, dealt chiefly with feats of manly strength
that he had witnessed; while the tailor and his
apprentice, who made periodical visits to Sillerton
to re-clothe the males of the village in new garments, retailed pretty much the gossip that they
gathered during their wanderings throughout
the country, and which, in those quiet times, when
"dailies" were yet undreamt of, were alike interesting to high and low, and young and old.

I had almost forgotten little Sandy Simms, the
cobbler, but I am now under the impression that
his forte lay in relating stories that very graphic-
ally brought out the pawky character of Scottish humor. But Jean operated in another field
altogether—the horrible in what was human, and

the blood-curdling in what was supernatural, being the commodities in which she dealt. Nor was her stock of these by any means limited, as kelpies, goblins, fairies, brownies, elves, ghosts, wizards, witches, and sundry others of a kindred nature, were to her household words. Had she been requested to describe these, I doubt not Jean would have done so with ease, and classified them to the entire satisfaction of the most exacting scientist. Then, in addition to melancholy songs and ballads, all invariably of a lugubrious character, and covering a wide field of weird literature, her vivid imagination, and her peculiar faculty of finding suitable words to express her meaning, would alone have made her remarkable in any community. To us she certainly was remarkable, and charmed us as the snake charms its unresisting prey.

Jean, along with her husband and family, occupied a small cottage in the village square of Sillerton. Her husband, the only Seceder, we believe, in the parish, we mean apart from a few members of the Episcopal Church, was wont on winter evenings to wend his way after supper to the house of a neighbor, where politics and religion were freely discussed. Jean was thus pretty much left to her own devices during the evening, and she employed her time thoroughly. I see that kitchen now, just as I used to see it fifty years ago. There is only an earthen floor, and apart from the dim light that is supplied by half a dozen smouldering peats, the only attempt at lighting the humble apartment is by a splinter of fir root stuck in a link of the crook or chain that hangs in the chimney, and as one of these primitive candles is consumed, another is lighted and put in its place.

As if by concert, at a certain hour every evening, the youngsters of the village congregate in Jean's kitchen. The few stools and benches, or deeces, more properly called, that were distributed round the kitchen are soon filled by the expectant crowd. But I had almost forgotten the seat of honor on these occasions. This was at the two opposite sides of the capacious chimney which stretched half across the gable of the house, and where three or four urchins could easily find both snug and ample quarters. These seats were, however, difficult to obtain, and were for two reasons much sought after by the audience. The first reason was, that on a cold winter night, there was a warmth there not to be found in any other part of the house, and the second was (we will own a somewhat peculiar one) that the occupants of these seats could not be attacked from the rear, and no matter what happened, they were comparatively safe in that quarter.

Jean Barden sits on, or rather in, one of these huge wooden four-poster chairs that have become fashionable again, but now wearing brighter colors than their more homely prototype. Without any preliminary remarks whatever, Jean commences her tale of the evening, and with little or no interruption, except from a renewal of a light that had burned out, or on account of a chip of fir that had accidentally fallen down, the tale goes on for at least an hour and a half.

At this distant date, I could not restore, so to speak, one story that Jean ever told, but there are certainly pieces of many of them that still cling tenaciously to the memory. Just read over the horrors that Tam O'Shanter saw in Alloa Kirk, and you will have a fair idea of the species of literature on which we feasted on those wintry nights.

One evening we had a ghost story in all its weird associations; a ghost that came and went like a gleam of light; some unquiet spirit perhaps that left the earth with some momentous secret upon its soul, and that was permitted to revisit scenes with which it was once familiar in the flesh, in order to communicate what it knew to some one bold enough to demand its errand.

At another time we had stories connected with troublous times when fire and sword swept even the peaceful Garioch; while occurrences of the "45" were reproduced, but all tinged with those shades of coloring that Jean's skilful hand knew so well how to apply.

Then, again, we had the account of some dreadful murder that had once been committed within the bounds. The circumstances are all laid before us; the culprit is described and produced in Court; the trial takes place once more; the prisoner is found guilty; the judge puts on the terrible black cap of doom; the ghastly gallows appears, and the tragedy ends with probably a few verses of a melancholy song that the unhappy man is supposed to have composed on the very morning of his execution, something, in fact, finding a counterpart in the Banff freebooter who

> "Played a tune and danced it roun'
> Beneath the gallows-tree."

As to robberies, they were numerous "as leaves in Vallombrosa," and had comparatively little interest unless some one was shot or knifed on the occasion. In fact, things of the ordinary class had no charms for us. Of dismal love-stories also there were not a few, and in all these cases the course never did run smooth. Stern fathers and unfeeling mothers arose to forbid the banns; there were insuperable difficulties that could not be got over, and in consequence, we had a whole school of "Mill o' Tiftie's Annies," and too frequently the conclusion poured forth the melancholy wail—

> "My true love died for me to-day;
> I'll die for him to-morrow."

In fact Jean's chamber of horrors would not have yielded to that of Madame Tussaud, and was different only in this, that the wax figure appealed simply to the eye, and was dumb, while Jean's brilliant imagination not only placed the individuals before the mental eye, but made each one tell his own tale. Truly the dry bones that Jean Barden laid before us did not long remain such. There was soon a shaking amongst them, and under her magic touch, they became clothed anew with all the outward appearances of animated life, and speedily found living tongues to record once more their own experiences.

There was also one peculiarity about many of Jean's ghost stories that gave them an interest that we could not otherwise have so keenly felt; they were localized and connected with places that we all knew well. In fact, there were few lonely places in the parish without some brownie, or fairy, or boodie of evil odor associated with it.

And there we sat and shivered, and listened with rapt attention while the story sped on its way; listened with mouths and eyes widely opened to drink in all the absorbing details; listened with a growing terror in our hearts at what might be, for all we knew, very near ourselves. And when the last word was spoken, and Jean, rising from her lecture chair, waved us to the door with the somewhat abrupt good night—"Noo, bairns, aff to bed," we scampered off like a flock of frightened sheep. None of us had very far to go, but short as was the distance that intervened between Jean Barden's kitchen and my father's house, I would rather have run the gauntlet between two lines of Indian braves, than traverse the few yards that I had to cover till I reached my own door. I fancied that there was a perfect host of malignant spirits behind me, with no running stream to bar pursuit. And so it happened, that as the paternal door closed behind me, I felt, only then, that I could breathe again in safety.

The question, indeed, might be asked, "But why listen to stories that produced such disagreeable consequences; why go when the returning was accompanied by such terrors as might have well kept us at home?" Alas! gentle reader, is it then hard to find an answer? Look at that poor bewildered

7

moth circling nearer and nearer the flame that at
last consumes its beauteous wings, and leaves it
scorched and helpless on the ground to die. And
has it never happened in your own experience, that
you have felt just like that scorched moth—not while
you were circling round your alluring light, but
when—wings and hope all gone—you felt scorched
and helpless?

We may not press the question further, for we
well know what the answer should be, were the
truth—the simple truth—the whole truth told.

And so with us poor youngsters. There was a
glamour about Jean Barden and her stories that we
could not resist, and night after night, and week
after week did we listen, until they became part and
parcel of ourselves. And what was the consequence? There was not a youth amongst us that
would have gone through the Home Park, or the
Howe o' Coghard, after nightfall, could he by so
doing have earned his weight in gold. Had we told
at home all that we had heard, it might have been
very different, but we evidently kept all this to ourselves. At the same time, in those days, there was
little censorship exercised over tales told in the
kitchen, and very probably there would have been
no alarm at the result, even had the whole been
known.

I shall now step into the witness-box, and to show the unwholesomeness of such milk as Jean ladled out to the youngsters of Sillerton, I shall honestly relate what I experienced on the very first trip that I made, after nightfall, and alone. I had been promised a pair of " Bantams," by a farmer living somewhere beyond Pitcaple—that is to say, about fifteen miles from Sillerton. On a bright summer morning during the harvest holidays I saddled my pony, strapped on my back a suitable basket, and started for the home of my Bantams, the name of which place I have forgotten. I reached the farm all right, but every one was engaged in harvest work in the distant fields, and so it happened that before I got my Bantams in my basket, and I was duly mounted on Donald's back, the sun had gone down and dark shadows were stealing along the sides and slopes of Bennachie.

There was not much very startling in this, but as I trotted on, the shadows grew darker, until I found that I had to find my way home over a good dozen Scotch miles, and in the dark. This was my first experience of such a trial, and I certainly felt it. When I arrived at Gaudy Ford, the river seemed to me to have risen since I passed during the day, and there was a noise of rushing waters that kept me pondering on the bank for some time. At last,

however, realizing the fact that home lay beyond
the ford, and recollecting that Donald could swim
well, and so could his master, I pushed on and
through, and found that the stillness of night and
the deep gloom had both combined to make things
look worse than they actually were.

Gaudy crossed and left behind, new troubles and
fresh horrors came. The road passed along the
base of Bennachie, and in many places, as I came
nearer Sillerton, I mean the boundaries of the parish,
it was approached on both sides by deep woods that
sometimes completely overshadowed it. Then there
were unearthly, uncanny sounds that fell harshly
upon the ear; the roe deer would occasionally make
a startled run from approaching footsteps, and the
short yap of the disturbed fox, as he scurried across
the road, had a most depressing effect upon my
spirits. Courage I had almost said, but no: all the
courage I once had had oozed out. It required a
supreme effort of the will to enable me to make any
progress whatever, even under the most ordinary
circumstances, and when more than ordinary dan-
gers seemed near—well, then, a shake of the basket
which started a cackle of the fowls huddled within
it, and a quiet but fervent repetition of the Lord's
Prayer, gave me renewed strength and backbone, and
I trotted on.

The Howe o' Coghard was my last painful experience on that eventful journey. Jean Barden had shown a special favor for this place, and brownies, witches, and warlocks—ghosts with heads and without them were there—sighs and sounds that seemed to come from another world were often heard there, and in fact a finer field for awe-inspiring, gruesome influences could scarcely be imagined. I felt all this keenly. The horrible stories associated with the place all rushed back upon a memory that was perhaps on this occasion too retentive, and cautiously I drew bridle before plunging into the dismal shades of Coghard.

The evening was now far spent. My progress had been unusually slow, as I had literally to often feel my way, and over and above the darkness of an autumn moonless night, there was an unpleasant sough among the tree-tops that threatened rain. There was, however, no help for it. I would have sooner joined a forlorn hope, and stormed a deadly breach, than ride that night through the Howe o' Coghard, but yet my home in Sillerton was beyond.

How that basket rattled on my back, how the Bantams cackled and protested, and how fervently my prayers were said, I cannot tell now, but with the encouragement derived from both, and a more than usually liberal use of the heel upon Donald,

the Howe was speedily and safely passed, and I soon
thereafter found myself in the village of Sillerton.

The same sensations I never again experienced.
I was during that solitary ride almost cured of my
superstitious weaknesses; Jean Barden's teachings
were, by a supreme, perhaps heroic effort, ignomin-
iously cast aside, and I then learned to laugh at
terrors, that have ere now turned some black heads
almost instantaneously white.

Jean, we doubt not, was honest in her convictions,
as far as they went, and plied her art to the end of
life, and doubtless was often thanked for the amusement she afforded the youngsters. I must say,
however, for myself, that had I learned that any
one had been indoctrinating my own young bar-
barians with such poison as I had personally sucked
in Jean Barden's fir-lighted kitchen in the village
of Sillerton fifty years ago, I would have said with
the genial author of the "Ewie wi' the Crookit
Horn"—

> "O! gin I had the loun that did it,
> Sworn I hae, as well as said it,
> Tho' a' the warld should forbid it,
> I wad gie his neck a thraw."

CHAPTER XIII.

THE POOR PRIOR TO THE POOR LAWS.

" For ye have the poor with you always."
ST. MARK, XIV., 7.

BEFORE Poor Laws were enacted, there existed a very primitive state of things as to those who were denominated the poor. I do not mean to say that there were really no paupers, but poverty, at least in country places, did not appear very oppressive.

Most people put forth an effort to aid in supporting their poor relations; the Kirk-Session sent, per the hands of the elders, a quarterly dole of a few shillings to gladden the hearts of the aged recipients; occasionally there were charities that provided a pittance for the deserving poor, and almost always, there were milk and meal, and perhaps a few things besides, that found their way from the farmhouse to the humble abodes of those who, in some respects, like the Russian serf, seemed to belong to the soil.

It should be mentioned, also, that one or two

channels there were, in addition to the means already stated, by which the old and indigent could eke out their somewhat contracted living, so that altogether the inevitably poor could manage to get the two ends to meet.

This chapter is headed " The Poor prior to the Poor Laws." This heading is selected advisedly, since my acquaintance with the poor, under the new system, dated several years later—in fact, after I had left college. That these laws were necessary there can be no doubt, but as little doubt is there, that, by their operation, a change for the worse was produced in the minds of the Scottish peasantry, and that honest pride, that stinted itself to keep a poor relative from becoming a charge on the parish, entirely died away, and, instead, the more matter-of-fact feeling crept in—" If I pay my public rates, then my private charity ceases."

With this brief explanation of the reason why I circumscribe my acquaintance with those requiring charity, I shall at once proceed with the subject more immediately before me, and show how much or how little I knew of the poor of Sillerton, before the Poor Laws were enacted for their benefit.

In close proximity to several of the large farms, there were one or two cottages occupied by aged people, who had, perhaps, in younger days, been employed as laborers on the farm. Did I say "cottages?" Well, that would be a misnomer. These dwellings were huts of the most primitive character, built of rough stones and sods, compacted together somehow; thatched with straw or heather, and with a floor made of clay that had received much the same treatment it would have got in a brick-yard, with the exception of the baking process, which, in this case, was never applied, the feet of the occupants and the footsteps of time being deemed sufficient to render this primitive floor fit for the purpose it was intended to serve. There was generally but one bole, or small window, looking out to the south; two windows being in order when the dwelling boasted a " but and a ben."

There was no ceiling in these simple abodes, and the wood or peat fires that burned upon large slab-stones that formed the hearth produced a smoke that curled gracefully among the blackened rafters, until it found its way out by a hole in the roof, that could scarcely be called by the respectable name of a chimney, but which, at the same time, did duty for that excellent institution.

I do not mean to insinuate in the slightest degree that these huts were not comfortable, and that their occupants were not quite contented with them; but they certainly had their drawbacks. In certain conditions of the weather the smoke seemed to get bewildered, and could not find its way to the usual place of exit, but then the occupants, like the traditional eels, were used to this pyroligneous tribulation, though I honestly confess that, to one unaccustomed to it, it would have been simply intolerable.

An old friend in Canada, who had amassed a large fortune, told me that he had once taken a holiday to go and visit his aged mother, who lived near the banks of the Spey. He was most anxious to spend a few days with the old lady, but was literally driven out of the house by the smoke, and had to take up his quarters in the hotel at Carr-Bridge, whence he could make occasional trips to visit her. Willingly would he have built a chimney, but the old woman demurred. That would have been an innovation that would have completely upset all her arrangements, and the son left his aged parent contented to live and die in the smoke.

Speaking of smoke in Scotland reminds me of an incident that once happened in Canada to a couple of officers of the Royal Engineers and your humble servant, then officiating chaplain for that distinguished corps, and on which occasion smoke played a conspicuous part. We had gone, during the bleak and stormy month of January, to shoot, " promiscuously," I may call it, in that primeval forest of yellow pine that then mantled the banks of the Chaudiere, and in which there then existed a paradise both for the sportsman and for the lumberman.

We were the guests of a member of the latter class, and spent three or four days, I should rather say nights, in one of his camps, which was built in what was once the hunting-grounds of the Abenaquais Indians, of whom only one family lived now in all that region.

That we were comfortable generally goes without saying. The old cook had once worn Her Majesty's uniform, and his heart warmed when he found that his guests were of the militant profession, whether clerical or otherwise, and every effort was put forth to render us as comfortable as gastronomic art could make us.

If pork and beans, the other luxuries that are to be found in a lumber camp, and the ordinary etceteras that we brought along with us, could make mortals happy, we had been happy indeed. But the Bubbly Jock was there, even in that primitive camp. The large "caboose" that occupied the centre of the shanty would persist in sending jets of smoke indiscriminately to every corner of the camp.

Had it been summer, and had the mosquitoes and other pests that then hold high holiday in Canadian

woods been in force, we might have submitted with
a good grace to the smudge that was constantly and
ruthlessly permeating our whole system. We held
a council of war; our highest scientific skill was
brought into play to devise a cure for the smoke
nuisance, and after mature deliberation we felt that
we could successfully grapple with and conquer our
enemy.

So far, so well. Peter Farley, the cook, was invited to join our caucus. He was shown the method
we proposed to employ, to get rid of the vile smoke
that was gradually lessening the distance between
us and the noble red man, and we dreamt in imagination—so fondly dreamt—of a few hours of serene,
unclouded happineess in that camp, and in our ex-
uberance of joy we asked Farley if we had not completely solved the difficulty.

Peter not for one moment hesitated. In his mind
the smoke question had been long solved, and it gave
him no trouble whatever to unfold his opinion on
the matter. "Well, gentlemen," said the ex-private
of Her Majesty's 16th Foot, and now chief cook of
Grande Roche Camp, "we are not in England, and
if you cure the smoke, there is no saying but that
some of the boys may find fault with the cooking."

Having delivered himself of this oracular response,
Farley left us to our own meditations, and quickly dis-

appeared in the commingling cloud of smoke and
steam that whirled and floated around and above the
blazing caboose. It was very evident to us that there
were other things that troubled more the anxious
cook than the vile pyroligneous acid that might pinch
the eyes or excite the choler of his sorrowful guests,
who verily had been gradually developing into a
species of human " weeping willows."

Our fate was undoubtedly sealed; from Peter's
judgment there was no appeal. Another twenty-
four-hours' rubbing in of this " Indian tan " would
make us as yellow as the mocassins that we wore,
and we simply bent to the inevitable. The very
rapid depletion of our cigar-cases within the next
half-hour, and the dense volume of tobacco-smoke
that rose above us and gradually joined issue with
the mightier cloud into which Farley had incon-
tinently disappeared, might have easily convinced
the most sceptical unbeliever, that the guests of the
genial proprietor of Grand Roche Camp were firm
believers in the great maxim of the homœopathists
— *Similia similibus curantur* — " Likes are cured
by likes."

To return to our Sillerton poor and their smoky
dwellings, we may remark, that, if they disregarded
the smoke, they were equally callous with regard to
the question of light. In fact, there came less light

from the miniature window than from the peat fire that smouldered on the hearth. But yet the occupants were contented therewith ; they did not really require much light; their duties inside were not of such a nature as to require the glare of an electric fifty-candle-power carbon-burner, and if additional light were necessary, it could readily be produced in a decidedly primitive way, namely, by sticking a lighted fir-spunk in a link of the crook that hung over the fireplace. In fact, they objected on principle to the enlargement of their windows.

On one occasion, along with my father, I visited an old man who lived somewhere near the old house of Tillyfour in such a hut as I have described.

James Marnoch was then upwards of a hundred years of age, but still retained all his faculties, and was quite able to care in every way for himself. In James's hut there was no window whatever, and all the light of heaven he received, he did so on the outside of his biggin', or in a subdued form down the chimney.

The Lady of Sillerton took much kindly interest in the poor of the parish, and provided many a little comfort for them that came in handy during the cold months of winter. Marnoch was one of her favorites, and generally received a visit from his benefactress occasionally during the summer.

Late in autumn she left for England, but before leaving, usually constituted my father her almoner, and to him entrusted whatever she had provided for her numerous pensioners, accompanied oftentimes with kindly messages, and hopeful wishes for their welfare.

To Marnoch, on this occasion, were handed sundry parcels containing clothing, tea, sugar, and many small yet necessary articles besides. To deliver these was an easy matter, but I observed that my father had evidently something else to communicate, but apparently he had some difficulty in broaching it. At last, out it came. He had received instructions to get a window placed in the hut, as an improvement that his benefactress doubtless thought would be heartily appreciated by the centenarian.

My father had doubts on that subject, and these were speedily confirmed. Marnoch expressed his grateful thanks for all the kindness received, but positively refused to accept the window. He had got accustomed to the light that came in by open door, or chimney, and more light would be disagreeable to him, and, in addition to this, the opening of a space for the proposed improvement might admit the cold as well as the light. James Marnoch lived and died in that hut, but no window was ever inserted in its wall.

One source of earning a few shillings now and then came to those poor creatures, at least to the women. in the way of knitting stockings and other clothing. There was always a demand for such articles amongst a class, that had neither the inclination nor perhaps the time to do such work, and where the small charge made was certainly a temptation to get the knitting done elsewhere than at home. But beyond the local trade, if I might so call it, there was a larger trade that found abundant employment for such as were able and willing to work.

An agent for some manufacturing firm, or firms, made periodical visits to Sillerton, on which occasions he supplied his knitters with yarn, and at the same time received from them the articles finished since his former visit. It is true that very small prices were allowed for such work, but yet what they received was to them a sort of " Godsend," and, after all, the work required made but little demand upon their time, and, in fact, it often appeared to me that the old " bodies " could go on with their knitting under any circumstances, and without any apparent effort whatever.

It is at least worthy of remark that no one protested against either the hardships undergone by the aged knitters of agency goods, nor against the meagreness of the pay received for the work done, and certainly no Sillertonian Thomas Hood arose to awaken the torpor of the rich by writing or singing "The Song of the Stocking." At all events, the amounts received, small as they were, doubtless procured a few of those creature comforts that age still permitted them to enjoy.

There were no weavers in Sillerton, but in some of the neighboring parishes, work was found for this class much in the same way as was done in the knitting department. Material was supplied by an agent, and the cloth returned to him when finished. It occasionally happened, however, that, for some fault in the weaving, the web was rejected, and the value of the material supplied for its manufacture had to be refunded by the unfortunate weaver.

I shall now close this chapter with an anecdote, the gist of which depends upon the custom above indicated. One day a well-known medical practitioner residing in the ancient burgh of Inverurie, while going his rounds, met an acquaintance, a weaver, who was returning from a disagreeable interview with the cloth agent, and carrying a rejected web under his arm. The doctor was not aware that Davie had made a failure, and cheerily remarked, "Weel, Davie, are ye gain' hame wi' your wark?" Davie fancied that the question was a piece of sarcasm on the doctor's part, and owed him one for it.

8

An opportunity soon offered. A patient of the doctor, in spite of all that science and care had done for him, went the way of all flesh. The funeral cortége was passing along the street on the way to the churchyard, and the doctor was walking behind the hearse with the sorrowing relatives. Davie chanced to be on hand, and saw, at a glance, that his opportunity had come. Rushing forward to the astonished medical practitioner, he bawled out, loud enough to be heard on both sides of the street, " Weel, doctor, are ye gain' hame wi' your wark?" putting great emphasis upon the possessive pronoun.

It was not long before the doctor took in the situation, and enjoyed it accordingly, and sitting at his hospitable table years afterwards, I had the privilege of hearing the story from his own lips. From the doctor's unqualified merriment, I presume that he was satisfied, in his own mind, that Davie's sarcasm was, at least on this occasion, unmerited.

CHAPTER XIV.

LICENSED BEGGARS—THE FATUOUS AND INSANE.

Angels and ministers of grace defend us !
                                        Hamlet.

In the last chapter, in stating what I knew about the poor before the poor laws were enacted, there was no mention made of any aristocracy of poverty in Sillerton. We had no Edie Ochiltrees there, no King's Bedesmen, no Blue Gowns—in fact no one exercising the right of asking charity within certain, or perhaps uncertain, bounds.

It was the fact, however, that there were individuals who travelled as professional beggars through many of the Aberdeenshire parishes, and who, doubtless, had obtained the privilege of doing so. I recollect the occasional visits to our village of two wandering paupers. One was called Dickey Daw, a poor harmless idiot, and her companion was a middle-aged female who solicited and collected means for their mutual support.

We had no analogous case in Sillerton, but such cases did exist in some of the neighboring parishes, and I have in my possession a document, issued by the kirk-session of Forbes, which will clearly enough show that such were perhaps common enough. The document referred to is as follows :—

These testify that the Bearer hereof Jean Bay, Sister to Isobel Bay, Spouse to Arthur Mitchell in the Parish of Forbes carries along with her Patrick Mitchell one of their children, of about five years of age, altogether deprived of the use of his Reason and Faculties of his Body ; and his Parents being reduced to Straitning Circumstances, and having other two young children incapable thro' Nonage to do anything for themselves, are obliged to employ the said Jean Bay the Child's aunt to supplicate and beg from charitable and well-disposed Persons for the said helpless objects Sustenance and Relief. Therefore the Kirk-Session of Forbes did, and hereby do, earnestly recommend the said Jean Bay to the Charity of all within the united Parishes of Forbes and through Burgh and Land, for her own and the said great Objects Relief : which in name and by appointment of the said Kirk-Session is attested at Forbes the twenty-ninth Day of December, One thousand seven hundred and fifty-six, by,

ALEXANDER OREM Moderator.
Alford Feb. 24th 1757.

That the Bearer the above named Jean Bay is really an Object of Charity, as having the Burthen of the above Arthur Mitchell's Children is attested by,

> ALEXANDER JOHNSTON Minister of Alford,
> PATRICK THOMSON Minister at Tough,
> WILLIAM MILNE Minister at Kildrummie,
> FRANCIS ADAM Minister at Cushny,
> THEODORE GORDON Minister at Kenethmont,
> PATRICK REID Minister at Clat.

The capital letters, commas, etc., are the same as

in the original. This licence to beg is duly printed on a tough, dark-colored paper, and very distinctly shows tear and wear. How long it was carried about through the vale of Alford and surrounding districts to advance the claims of Patrick Mitchell and others I know not; either the imbecile boy or his devoted nurse may have died in the parish of Sillerton, and the certificate alone remained to show the miserable parochial provision existing in Scotland in the year of grace 1756 for her fatuous poor.

Such documents are still issued in the province of Quebec, but lacking generally the formality of the Scotch one. May we draw the inference, that we are here, in some things at least, more than a century behind the civilization of Aberdeenshire? So much, then, for our duly accredited poor.

There were, however, two classes besides, who did not seem to dovetail into the general order of things. The fatuous, or "feels," as they were generally called, but not imbeciles like Patrick Mitchell, had no special place in our eleemosynary system, and led a somewhat peculiar life, wandering from place to place in search of their daily bread.

There was little to blame here, as generally this class was not by any means dangerous, and, in some slight respect gave, in the amusement they afforded, a species of return for what they had received, while their way of living entailed little, if indeed any, hardship whatever.

As an example of this, there was one individual of this class, one par excellence, who periodically visited Sillerton, "feel Jamie Nuckel," as the folks called him. I fear Jamie was more rogue than fool, and stood head and shoulders, in cunning and perhaps intellect of some kind, over his wandering confrères. Jamie had a most retentive memory, and was accustomed to repeat, almost verbatim, sermons that he had once heard. This faculty was a source of unbounded pleasure to the farm-servants on a winter evening, whenever Nuckel made his appearance, and the reward was just as much brose as Jamie could get under his belt.

On one occasion, however, his prowess in brose-consuming nearly ended in disaster. The modicum of brose provided for him was something almost incredible, and Nuckel broke the record. But he also almost broke something beside, as my father's men, who had given the dose as a test case, had to roll the glutton on the floor for a considerable time before he was considered safe from an explosion that might have proved fatal.

Jamie's cry on this occasion was very touching, "Row me or I'll rive, boys." He was rolled most effectually. That was his last sermon and feast there, for orders were given—and these orders had to be obeyed—that the experiment was not to be repeated, and many a time I have seen him as he passed, turning a longing look askance at the bothies of Fusselbare, where he had so often enjoyed a square meal, but his borrowed eloquence was no longer in demand in that quarter; the meal, butter, and boiling water were never again mixed for him, and Fusselbare knew Nuckel no more.

It may be well to state here that Nuckel was an exaggerated specimen of what the Poor Laws would now place under the heading of "fatuous," and that there were many different varieties of the same species, ranging from the unmitigated idiot, to individuals who wanted only "tippence of the shilling."

It is a matter of doubt if the "crank" might not be a connecting link, and if he might not be accurately classed between the feel and the madman. It is no matter of doubt, however, that we are now getting on dangerous ground, and that a return to our mutton might be advisable.

Of those who scored a few points below the ordinary standard of full reasoning powers, one, Sandy Forbes, carried a private mail-bag, to and from the post-office of Sillerton. It would be diffi-

cult to specify precisely what Sandy wanted, and I
might be better understood if I said, "Just a little
of everything."

Both in body and mind there was a want. One
said that Sandy's fingers were "a' thooms;"
another asserted that he scuttled in his walk, "like
a fluke;" and unquestionably he had a stutter in
his speech. As to his mental equipment, there was
a general haziness in every department. And yet
Sandy was a useful enough member of society. He
was good-natured, and willing to work, so far as
his capabilities went.

But it was chiefly as postman that Sandy was
employed. He not only carried the letters to and
from the post-office, which was also the village
store, but he was universally employed along the
road to bring small purchases with him on his return. These small orders amounted sometimes to
a very great number, but neither cash nor orders
embarrassed him; he wrote nothing down, and yet
goods and cash were always right, while no order
was ever under any circumstances forgotten.

Sometimes it happened that Sandy had been sent
in another direction, and a substitute had to be sent
instead, and as usual, came orders and cash from
every farmer and cottar's wife along the roadside.
But what a reckoning was there on the return trip!

Orders were entirely forgotten, or changed, or delivered in the wrong quarter; the guidwife of Pitfuffie found two ounces of tobacco where she expected the same quantity of tea; Johnny Wright's snuff turned out to be ground ginger that was sorely missed by a dyspeptic invalid farther on the road, who received a pound of three-inch nails instead; and in no case could the cash be brought to an exact balance.

The only thing that did really seem to tally, was the universal remark made with considerable bitterness, but only when the spurious postman had got at least a good hundred yards away—"I wish the peer feel, Sandy Forbes, had gane to the post instead of that gype." Here again nature seemed once more to make up in one direction what she had withheld in another, and where judgment was sadly deficient, memory was supplied with a greater liberality.

I am here reminded of an anecdote that I heard told by one who was intimately acquainted with the folk-lore of the Garioch, and who was wont to amuse many a Sillerton dinner-party therewith. The anecdote related to a family connected with the parish, and showed the difficulty that sometimes existed of determining the mental condition of an individual.

A doubt had arisen whether the heir-at-law of a certain estate could be considered perfectly sane or not, and this for legal reasons. He had been guilty of no outrage against the ordinary decencies and conventionalities of society, and he was quiet and retiring in his manner, but yet legal forms required to be satisfied.

A species of jury met to inquire into his mental condition, and took evidence accordingly. Several witnesses, for and against, were examined, as there were conflicting interests involved, and at length the defendant himself was brought before the Court. Several questions were put to him, all of which he answered with sufficient clearness, and the impression was growing that the verdict must be given in his favor.

Tiring of the questioning, however, to which he had been subjected, he slightly lost his temper, and asked the Court to hurry up, as the cattle would not be housed till he got home! The remark was fatal, and turned the scale that was inclining somewhat to his own side. The incongruity of the heir of an ancient house acting as cow-boy was to his judges clear enough evidence of mental weakness. The verdict was accordingly given in favor of plaintiff, and the self-appointed cow-boy lived to a good old age, but never entered upon the possession of his inheritance, and remained divested of the right and power of managing his own affairs.

Of the two undesirable classes I have mentioned, the "feel" has now been described as the representative of the one, and I shall now pass on to the "lunatic," as representing the other.

It is a strange thing to think of, yet not stranger than true, that lunatics, pure and simple—lunatics in every sense of the word—were, many of them at least, at large in " Bonnie Scotland " about fifty years ago; not the merely fatuous, but even those who, if not admitted to be normally dangerous, might become so at any moment. Of course a wild raving maniac had to be looked to, and stone walls, and the never-failing strait-jacket, either restored the equilibrium of mind that seemed to have been disturbed, or provided another unfortunate for the funeral, where there was little sorrowing, and but few tears.

The connecting link was certainly a very peculiar being, quiet generally and inoffensive, and able to speak discreetly on every subject except one; but no sooner was that one mentioned than all rationality fled, and the monomaniac came at once to the front. Examples of this class are often to be met with, but in Sillerton there was certainly a very peculiar variety of the species.

James, or rather Jamie Muir, was a fine, strong, well-built chiel; able to attend to any ordinary duties, and possessed of a garden that was the admiration of the whole country-side. But Jamie was literally mad on tartans. Whether he had got the idea that he was descended from some great Highland chief, I could never learn, but on all marked occasions, when the good folks of Sillerton met for festive or other purposes, there was Muir in full Highland costume, and sporting a bonnet and feather that might have passed muster before a Field-Marshal.

One other peculiarity Jamie had; he made a practice of climbing to the top of the tallest trees in the parish, and always left a small flag of tartan fluttering from the topmost bough. On one occasion he slipped when leaving his loftiest perch, but as the tree was a larch, the branches drew out, so to speak, as Jamie's weight came upon them, and when he arrived, or nearly arrived, at terra firma, he lay upon half a cartload of branches, and the stately tree was completely stripped on one side.

Jamie was considerably flurried on this occasion, but a huge pinch of sneeshin' put him all right again. Nor did the accident wean him from his dangerous proclivities. Jamie was still to be seen amongst the branches, like the Pigmies of Darkest

Africa, and his small flags still fluttered mast-high over his favorite trees.

His brother was, however, an entirely different character. Dark in appearance—solitary and unsociable in his disposition, and imbued with melancholy ideas with regard to most religious subjects, Willie Muir had more than once been placed under restraint, and had returned home, only after long intervals of absence. No one imagined that he was really dangerous, but yet there was a general desire to shun him.

On these occasions, when it was evident that the disease, if disease it was, was growing on him, Willie, or rather mad Willie Muir, as he was commonly called, was often to be seen passing through the little village, always bareheaded, and generally with a ponderous cudgel in his hand.

On one of these occasions, instead of passing through the village, as was his wont, he made at once for the parish school, and opening the door suddenly, stood before the terrified youngsters, and, if possible, the more terrified schoolmaster. Looking neither to the right hand nor to the left, he made direct for the bench where sat Marshal Graham, one of the biggest boys in the school, and probably one of the most self-possessed.

" Marshal Graham ! " roared the madman, " take

up your Bible there; turn up the fifth chapter of
Mark, and read it before me, roun' the village
square; and if ye miss ae word or letter, aff gaes
yer head, like a carl doddie!" The carl doddie was
one of those heavy-headed grasses with which we
played some game of chance, by knocking off the
heads against each other.

Up rose Graham, without one moment's hesitation
—took his Bible in his hands, duly turned up the
chapter as directed, and quietly awaited further
orders. With a quiet but firm grip upon the collar
of the jacket, Muir speedily put Graham in march-
ing order at the door of the school.

But before the Scripture reading began, there was
a preparation on the part of the madman that
utterly terrorized the whole community. Muir
deliberately drew from his pocket a razor, evidently
prepared for the occasion, and brandishing this
several times before Graham's eyes, ordered him to
proceed.

During all this time, which, after all did not extend beyond a very few minutes, the poor dominie
seemed dumfounded and helpless, but as Muir and
his Scripture reader marched away from the school
door, he suddenly seemed to recover his senses, and
escaping from one of the windows that opened towards the back, made for the manse as if a thousand

fiends were behind him. Luckily, quiet, gentle Fordyce was in his garden, and though a peculiarly retiring and indeed timid man, he yet at once went
with the still more timid schoolmaster to the rescue
of Graham.

But how progressed the reading all this time?
Slowly yet firmly, Graham marched round the village square reading aloud the prescribed passage,
with Muir following closely behind him, listening
eagerly to the words as they fell from the boy's lips
and watching if there was any divergence from the
authorized text, for mad Willie Muir knew the passage most accurately, and would, no doubt, have
visited an error with instant and terrible punishment.

There was something supremely awful in the
madman's look as he stalked behind that almost
doomed boy, and brandished the weapon of punishment in his hand. Once had the square been gone
over, yet the chapter was only half read, and the
weird ordeal went on. At that hour there was
scarcely a man in the village, and if man there was,
he certainly made no sign. The terror-stricken
urchins did not dare to approach the scene openly,
but from nooks and corners watched the progress
of the reader and his judge.

Ah! might not that judge at any moment have

developed into the grim finisher of the law; while many a blanched face peeped out cautiously from the windows as the procession moved along, dreading at every instant lest the final tragedy might come.

On still went Graham and Muir, till the square was circled for the second time, and just at that point, as the minister and the schoolmaster reached the group, Graham's voice clearly and correctly repeated the concluding words of the chapter.

There was an ominous pause, only for a second or two, and then the madman's voice uttered a responsive " Amen." The unexpected appearance on the scene of the clergyman, whom Muir had been ever taught to respect, seemed to act like a sedative upon his troubled mind, and slowly the open razor was closed and placed in his pocket. With admirable tact, Fordyce forebore to revert to the cause that had brought him so unexpectedly to the village square, and, as he made some commonplace remarks that at once attracted Muir's attention, the sorely-tried but successful scripture-reader at once took in the situation, and quietly placing a few yards between himself and the trio, suddenly put on a spurt that has probably seldom been beaten.

There was no meeting again that day in the parish school of Sillerton. The dominie was considerably demoralized, and the scholars had witnessed a scene that might have well driven Latin, and English grammar, and everything else completely out of their heads for even longer time than an afternoon. At all events, neither teacher nor taught entered again that day the school, and it was a long time before it ceased to be remembered what the occasion was that gave a half-holiday to the children of Sillerton.

Mad Willie Muir had to be put once more under restraint, and never again returned to the parish. It was generally said that on his recovery he emigrated to America, while a few were wont to relate on social occasions, when talk and toddy flowed freely together about the village inn, that they had reason to believe that Muir was eventually devoured by grizzly bears among the " Rockies " of the then "Far West."

Be that as it may, we believe that some social Scottish customs have been changed for the better, and that there is no great chance now of any youngster of Sillerton being paraded to read a Scripture lesson with a raving madman at his side, and with the suggestive accompaniment of an open razor blazing ominously before or behind him.

9

CHAPTER XV.

CONVIVIALITIES OF SILLERTON.

Wi' merry sangs an' friendly cracks,
  I wat they didna weary ;
An' unco tales an' funnie jokes,
  Their sports were cheap an' cheery.

Halloween.

IT is undoubtedly a relief to pass from the company of fools, monomaniacs, and madmen to almost any other society whatever. But yet most of our pleasures are founded on contrast, or at least intensified by it.

The poet has not forgotten to remind us that "Sweet is pleasure after pain," and we scarcely require to go to the poet to become convinced of this truism. We seem to fall in love on some principle of contrast; the grave not unfrequently affect the company of the gay ; learned Lords of Session have, in more than one instance, taken to themselves wives whose chief education consisted in the ability to roast a joint or broil a beefsteak ; while how often have we seen a veritable giant of six feet and a few inches over, striding along with a wife hanging on his arm who might have passed for a first cousin of one of Gulliver's Liliputians!

Probably it was the force of contrast that induced the comely Scotch lassie to marry, and who, when asked by a neighbor, "Fat made ye marry that ugly chiel?" very innocently replied, "Weel I wat, he's nae a beauty, but then he's sic a guid-natured breet."

Well, from the grave things discussed in last chapter we would now take a glance at those social amusements that occasionally and sometimes periodically engaged the attention of the good folks of Sillerton.

No better description of the lively game of football, as practised by the boys and hobbledehoys of the parish, could we give than that supplied by the author of "Tullochgorum," but alas! few Scotchmen now would get through a verse without looking into Jamieson at least a dozen of times, and I much fear, I will scarcely be held to have thrown much enlightenment upon the subject by quoting the following stanza :—

> " Like bumbees bizzing frae a byke,
>   When herds their riggins tirr,
> The swankies lap thro' mire and syke,
>   Wow as their heads did birr !

> " They youff'd the ba' frae dyke to dyke
>   Wi unco speed and virr ;
> Some baith their shou'ders up did fyke,
>   For blythness some did flirr
>   Their teeth that day."

Then we had our Halloween, not perhaps with all the different ingredients that Burns with artistic hand has thrown into his wonderful poem, but yet we had many of these, as well as those grand bonfires, that in our young days lighted up every hill and brae from Aberdeen to the Moray Firth, for this much we could discern from the Mither Tap o' Bennachie ; how much farther north I cannot say.

Then came genial Yule with all its wealth of fun and jollity, and Auld New Year's Day, that we all sat up to greet, with its lucky or unlucky "first foot," its inevitable whisky bottle, its sowens, both for the comfort of the inner man and for the ruin of the door of him who had perhaps weakly allowed sleep to steal upon him, and so forgot his midnight vigil; those shooting matches that gave a deeper zest to the ploughman's holiday; and last, though not least, on high occasions, the grand ball in some public hall, or perhaps barn, swept and garnished for the nonce, and where high and low met on a common platform, where all went merry as a marriage bell, and ordinary jealousies and social differences were forgotten, at least until next morning's sun threw into shade the tallow dips that still flared and spluttered on the wall.

Then what of our weddings and christenings? Were they not social events well deserving of commemoration? Who could express a doubt who mingled in our merry-makings fifty years ago, perhaps less? The christening had, of course, its higher religious associations, but it had its social side as well, and the genial parson, as a rule, when he concluded one part, was by no means averse to mingle in the other, the fact being that in Scotland, and indeed amongst Scotchmen wherever located or domiciled, the minister's duty was only half performed when the child was duly enrolled a Christian, and at the social board thereafter, his carving knife required as fine an edge as his tongue possessed before grace was said.

I cannot deny myself the pleasure of here repeating an anecdote that I got from one of the fathers of the Church of Scotland in Canada. Would that I could reproduce the very words and gestures that gave such reality to the story!

The scene was laid in Scotland, where a knowledge of the Shorter Catechism was supposed to be the property of every man, woman and child belonging to the Kirk, and where regular diets of catechis-

ing were held throughout every parish at stated
times by the parish minister. A parishioner called
upon his minister to request him to come and christen
his first-born. The minister consented, but took
the liberty, as was his duty, of asking John one or
two questions in the Catechism that touched more
particularly upon the question of baptism.

John was found wanting, so far as knowledge on
this subject was concerned, and the conscientious
parson put off the christening to a more convenient
season—in fact until John should call a second time
at the manse, and prove that his knowledge of things
sacred was on the increase. John duly came, but
alas! no increase of knowledge came with him, and
still the minister refused to name the baptismal day.
In vain John pleaded that his brother and his
brother's wife and various relatives had been invited,
and could not decently be put off. But all in vain:
the parson was obdurate. The baptism had to be
delayed; the invited guests had to wait a little
longer, and John had to compear at the manse again
" on approbation."

Once more John came, but frail memory refused
still to repeat the information that the Catechism
gave, and on which his wife had most perseveringly
coached him, and the minister was, if possible, more
obdurate than ever. John pressed the point hard;

invited friends would be offended, and in fact insulted, and all that sort of thing. But no; the christening must be still delayed for reasons previously given.

At last a happy thought struck the parishioner, and he at once unburdened himself of his secret. " Weel, minister, I may jist tell you the truth. Oor freens micht be put aff, bit, ye see, I hae bocht the whisky, and ye ken yoursel' that whisky winna keep."

My venerable friend did not enter into the whole scope of the argument that John so deftly handled, nor shall I either, but taking into account all the circumstances of the case, and after carefully coaching his somewhat obtuse pupil in his lesson, the worthy divine saw fit to shorten the term of purgatorial trial through which his parishioner was passing; the christening was duly celebrated at the time desired, and friends and whisky were both there.

As to how the good folks of Sillerton celebrated their weddings, I presume there was little difference between them and any other folks from " Maidenkirk to John o' Groats." That little difference consisted, I believe, in a shortening of the time, which must have been a happy relief to the newly-married couple, who, in those primitive days and places, did not start immediately after the " déjeuner à la fourchette," to spend their honeymoon amongst strangers, but who began to dispense the duties and graces of hospitality immediately after the nuptial knot had been tied.

There was, of course, the usual feet-washing the night before, and all the fun connected with the performance of that preliminary portion of the marriage service, and shared in chiefly by the nearer relatives and more intimate friends; there was the gathering at the bride's home of the invited guests; the bride in all the glory that such an occasion could supply; the groom scarcely knowing whether he stood on his head or heels; the bridesmaids and groomsmen wearing white gloves, and wondering what was their duty to do next; and the parson, duly robed for the occasion, and presiding not only in the more sacred part of the service, but also in the merrymaking that followed the conclusion of the ceremony.

And then what fun and frolic came! How the tables verily groaned beneath the toothsome burdens that they bore! What genial and humorous speeches were delivered as the fumes of the exhilarating toddy rose to the very ceiling of the banquetting room! What sly wit and pawky humor flowed in one continuous stream from the sharpened tongues of the merry guests; and at last, how the younger members of the community enjoyed the concluding scene of the evening's performance—if indeed three or four o'clock in the morning could be so designated —when the bride's stocking was thrown among the revellers, and happy was the lad or lass that had the good fortune to catch it! Their turn undoubtedly came next.

Yet, all the marriage festivities were comprised within two rounds of the clock in Sillerton, though farther north the celebration of a marriage sometimes occupied nearly a week, and came to a close, only when provisions and mountain dew were both exhausted.

A near relative of mine had the privilege of witnessing a wedding a hundred miles or so north of Sillerton, where the ceremonies were all conducted in Gaelic, where the ordinary conversation was kept up in that language, except occasionally when English was employed in deference to the groom and his best man, who both spoke the Doric of the Garioch, and that only, and where my friend escaped matrimony, at least on that occasion, by what is sometimes called a "close shave." I shall allow him to tell his story in his own way :—

"On one memorable occasion I witnessed a wedding on the banks of the Dulnan. A lad from Sillerton had found his fate beyond the Spey, and I was induced to accompany him to the home of his

bride. It was a long and weary road from a few
miles south of Bennachie till Craigellachie and the
Haughs of Cromdale passed, we crossed the swift-
flowing Spey near Grantown, and pushed onward in
the direction of the famed Aviemore. About three
in the morning, in the month of May, we came in
sight of our destination, but even at that uncanny
hour there were no eyes closed at Carr-Bridge. One
would have thought from appearances that the
Prodigal Son had arrived, and that at least a dozen
fatted calves had been sacrificed to welcome him.
The feast had already begun, and music and dancing
held high holiday.

"A most cordial reception was accorded us; Oriental hospitality could scarcely have surpassed in
any way the welcome that met us on the banks of
the Dulnan, and though the language of Ossian was
not quite so familiar to us as the Doric Scotch that
we had learned not far from where 'The Gadie rins
at the back o' Bennachie,' yet we felt, and had every
reason to feel, that we were highly honored guests.

"Resisting all temptations to indulge in a Highland fling, we soon sought the seclusion of our own
rooms, and had the whole and entire company of
the 'Jolly Beggars' been rehearsing their celebrated
cantata in the adjoining apartment, we would have
remained as oblivious of their very existence as if

our own mothers had rocked us to sleep. Soon—too
soon for us—the morning dawned—dawned, I mean,
when the shutters were removed—and the sun's
rays proved that Old Sol had beaten us by at least
a couple of hours.

"A perfect *feu de joie* was being fired within an
easy distance of our windows; about as many pipers
as the famous Fershon paraded to conquer and rav-
age the Clan MacTavish seemed to be tuning their
instruments in the immediate vicinity, and as your
humble servant was groomsman, and deeply ven-
erated the immortal Nelson's signal, 'England ex-
pects every man to do his duty,' we were soon ready
for action.

"What I or anybody else did on that memorable
occasion seems to have slipped almost entirely from
my recollection. I know that the old Celtic parson
persisted in mistaking me for the groom. I had in
fact joined hands with the blushing bride, at his
urgent request, thinking that this was probably the
right thing for the best man to do in the land of the
Grants, until a kindly hand forbade the banns, and
I at once took second place, but when that marriage
commenced or ended, I am not quite prepared to
say.

"About a week after, I had a most exciting search
after my Lowland garments, having evidently donned

the garb of old Gaul at a very early stage of the proceedings; and found to my surprise, by examining sundry documents that had been placed inside my sporran, that I had proposed to, and had been accepted by, over a dozen young ladies of the Strath.

"This, to me, was a somewhat startling revelation, and as I was not quite prepared to explain my peculiar position to all the stalwart fathers and brothers who might very soon be attempting to interview me, I beat a very precipitate retreat homewards, and as soon as possible, Craigellachie and Bennachie were by and by placed between me and the enemy.

"I am not quite sure why I, on this occasion, forgot so far my usual caution. It may have been the demoralizing influence of the unseemly hours we kept; perhaps it may have been produced by the extraordinary stimulating nature of the mountain air in the neighborhood of the classic Spey. At all events I never attended another wedding within a day's march of Rothiemurchus; the more staid and sober customs of a marriage in the Garioch were, like Artemus Ward's old flag, good enough for me.

"I have, ever since that famous time, firmly believed in the adage, that it is unwise for the shoemaker to go beyond his last. Nay more, I had theorized upon the proverb, and began to think that it might be better for Sillerton bachelors to keep to Sillerton belles, and if I ever again consent to aid and abet a friend in entangling himself in the nuptial noose, I shall insist on a Garioch celebration, and will personally appear rather in decent Garioch continuations, than befool myself in assisting to perform the same function arrayed in the garb of old Gaul, with a Gaelic Psalm or Pibroch or Coronach, or something of that sort, ringing in my ears, and that too a hundred miles nearer the North Pole than I should be."

Such was the account that my friend gave me of his experiences at a wedding on Speyside. It will no doubt provoke a smile, his difficulty in finding a good reason for his forgetting so many circumstances connected with the celebration, as also his forgetting his Lowland caution so much as to enter into love engagements wholesale and retail. No doubt the pure air that was wafted to the Strath from the snowy heights and heath-clad sides of Cairngorm and Benmachdhui might have had an exhilarating effect upon a Garioch Scotsman, but there might have also been other causes.

I once was one of twelve, who celebrated the opening of salmon-fishing on the crystal waters of the Dee by a capital dinner in one of those hotels on Deeside, that were common enough in my young

days, and where nothing was wanting, in the way
of either solids or liquids, to make every one as happy
and contented as mortals may be. Of course,
amongst many other luxuries, the "Salmo Salar"
played a conspicuous part.

Many good stories of the rod and reel were told;
and a few good fishing songs were sung, and could
the gentle Izaac have revisited the earth, he would,
I flatter myself, have felt perfectly at home amongst
us. It is almost needless to say that at due intervals the small thistle circled rapidly round the table,
and that after the walnuts and the wine had run
their course, the rest of the evening was mainly devoted to the mixing of those ingredients, that in
days of old accompanied and closed every entertainment.

What we brewed or drank on that occasion I shall
not specify precisely, but may simply state, that not
particularly long before sunrise we all wended our
way, to our respective homes. Next day we met by
special appointment, and it seemed that every one
had some ailment that last evening's dinner had
given him—not anything very serious or dangerous,
but sufficient to place him below "par."

The salmon had disagreed with the digestive or-
gans of several; the pudding had been disastrous
to a few more, and one or two lamented that they

never indulged in cheese without proving martyrs to their indiscretion the following day.

One thing struck me as very peculiar, namely, that none for a moment suspected that the very liberal allowance of barley bree that they had consumed had any hand in their troubles. And yet, after all, I strongly suspect, that had a jury given a verdict upon the evidence before them, the fish, pudding, and cheese would have been declared innocent, and that a true bill would have been found against John Barleycorn. Is it possible that the peat-reek had anything to do with my friend's peculiar conduct on the banks of the Spey? I presume, after all, that the exhilaration was more due to its potency than to even the pure air of the Strath.

Times, doubtless, have changed now, but the last time I spent a few days in that quarter of the globe, a guest at the hospitable shooting quarters of a world-renowned English brewer, the first vision of the morning was the head-keeper with some genuine mountain dew to " wash down," as he said, " the cobwebs that had accumulated during the night." When a sportsman got wearied beyond his strength, breasting the rocks and braes in pursuit of the oftentimes wild and scared red grouse, the same panacea was at hand with the remark that one spur in the head was better than two in the heel; and the last thing at night was the liquid and aromatic night-cap—unfailing herald of that sweet and unbroken slumber, that in those days, or perhaps nights we should say, we never missed. Ah! well may we say with the old Roman Burns—

Tempora mutantur, et nos mutamur in illis.

CHAPTER XVI.

OTHER SILLERTON AMUSEMENTS—THE SOCIETY OF GARDENERS.

I hear them still, unchanged—though some from earth
Are music parted, and the tones of mirth—
Wild, silvery tones, that rang through days more bright!
Have died in others, yet to me they come,
Singing of boyhood back—the voices of my home!

HEMANS.

WERE it for no other reason than to look up the old records of the parish, I would fain revisit Sillerton. But what records, after all, could I look into, except those of the kirk-session, and I scarcely think that I would find there anything like a paragraph headed, "One of the amusements of Sillerton."

I might find the record, carefully and circumstantially told, of grave offences against the laws of the kirk, and morality in general; I might learn, if I did not know before, how the kirk-session dealt with transgressors, who certainly in those days "found their ways hard;" well and faithfully would I find it recorded that some incorrigible black sheep had to occupy the "cutty stool," or seat of repent-

10

ance, sometimes for many consecutive Sundays, and receive the public rebuke of the stern minister, and the sour and unrelenting looks of many an old saint, who had himself, perchance, turned over a new leaf, and, clothed in his robes of self-righteousness, had forgotten the warning, "Judge not, that ye be not judged."

Sitting at that session table, now many years ago, not as judge or jury, but as a simple scribe wielding not the tongue but the pen; listening to sobs that came from the very depths, and seeing tears that did not merely trickle, but freely flowed over young, yet careworn cheeks, my thoughts wandered back to that grand old Temple of Jerusalem, whose greatest glory was, that it saw Him who came to carry back the wandering lambs to the sheep-fold.

A woman, bowed down with grief, and perchance remorse, bends before One who traces letters on the sand, indicating probably the ease with which records of sin might or should be blotted out, and utterly disregarding the stern faces that accused their frail sister, and demanding a judgment upon her sin. At length a voice says—"He that is without (this) sin, let him cast the first stone at her."

The shaft has struck home, and one by one her accusers silently steal away. When the Saviour looks up, none but the accused is there, and tenderly come the words from His gentle lips—" Neither do I condemn thee. Go, and sin no more."

Ah! how much more kindly was that erring one dealt with in the Jewish temple, than many an erring but repentant sinner in the auld kirk of Sillerton!

Such scenes would, unbidden, flit before my mind, and refuse to be driven away. They relentlessly left the stamp of an iron heel upon my soul; they came to stay, and with little effort I can recall, alas! too many of them still.

Well, I might, and certainly would, find recorded, tersely and coldly, such scenes as I have hinted at, but of any mere worldly amusements, or things of that nature, no, not one line.

And yet Sillerton had its gala days, when the parish put on its best looks, and work was pretty much at a standstill. There, for example, was the one great Fair that came once a year to gladden the hearts of not only the Sillertonians, but those of the neighboring parishes as well. There was, however, an object in the great annual Fair. Farmers gathered from all quarters to buy and sell; servants were engaged for the coming half-year and received the "arles" that were as binding nearly as the Queen's shilling. Jockey was able to buy ribbons to tie up Jeannie's "bonnie brown hair;" quarrels between rivals in the paths of love or war were either settled over a few glasses of Sillerton whisky, or decided with gloveless hands, in a fight to the finish, and according to some rules well-known to all, and which probably formed the basis of the Marquis of Queensbury's rules; and last, but not least, the annual Fair gave the boys and girls that usually attended the parish school of Sillerton a full and genuine holiday.

We can readily see the "why" and "wherefore" in all this, but in the case of the great annual meeting and grand parade of the Sillerton Gardeners, I was never able to fathom the cause of their existence in any shape whatever. This society, if it might be so called, is amongst the shadows of the past, and it requires some effort to recall it very clearly.

Like the shadows whose hands Æneas attempted to grasp in Hades, and who eluded him like a flitting dream, so appear now these shadowy Gardeners to me. As Wordsworth has it in his "Laodamia":

" Forth sprang the impassioned Queen her Lord to clasp ;
  Again that consummation she essay'd ;
But unsubstantial form eludes her grasp
  As often as that eager grasp was made."

And yet all is not mere shadow, and some figures rise above the ordinary level, like hilltops over a fog-covered landscape. The origin, however, and some other points connected with the Gardeners' Society of Sillerton, for a society it was really named, must remain, I fear, in profound obscurity. It is likely enough that when Sillerton Paradise was planned, and became an accomplished fact, with life-size figures of Adam and Eve, half-hidden amongst the yew-tree branches, the Gardeners may have been organized to represent some visiting committee of good or evil.

This, at all events, I do know, it was at least no benefit society, but the funds and dues collected at the annual parade were simply transferred from the pockets to the stomachs of the Gardeners, the expenses of the annual dinner requiring all the funds on hand, and rendering a cash account quite unnecessary.

This parade took place, I believe, about midsummer, at any rate when flowers were in their highest perfection, and in the village and neighborhood there were great preparations made for the gathering. Floral designs were then in order, and to our juvenile imaginations it seemed very wonderful, what the artistic talent of Sillerton could produce in that line. These designs were all ready the

evening before, and made their appearance only
when the floral warriors were ready to march.

At last the eventful day dawned. There was a
distant sound of music, if not of revelry; the brass
band of Oldmeldrum weavers had been engaged for
the occasion, and scouts, who were out in force on
such an exciting time, reported that the musicians
had already crossed at Boaty's Ferry, and were
now approaching the village in full blast. It would
be difficult to say whether the cattle in the Druid
Park or the youngsters of the village were the more
impressed and delighted.

I use the expression advisedly, for surely if
dolphins could be charmed by the lyre of Orpheus,
the bovines of Sillerton became equally susceptible
of pleasing impressions at the brazen blasts of the
Oldmeldrum weavers. And there in the village
square stood the venerable Gardeners with flowers
and banners and spears ready to receive them.

The author of the " Siller Gun " must have had
such a vision before his mind's eye when penning
the lines :

> " But ne'er, for uniform or air,
>   Was sic a group reviewed elsewhere !
> The short, the tall ; fat folk and spare ;
>   Syde coats, and dockit,
> Wigs, queues, and clubs, and curly hair;
>   Round hats, and cockit !

Wi' that the dinlin drums rebound,
Fifes, clarionets, and hautboys sound !
Through crowds on crowds, collected round,
    The Corporations
Trudge off, while Echo's self is drowned
    In acclamations !

Whether there was a special costume besides the
aprons that the members wore, and on which a nude
Adam and Eve, the Serpent, and an apple-tree in
full bearing, were all depicted in the most cunning
sampler stitch that the parish maidens could supply,
I know not; but there was one figure there that I
remember as if I had seen him only yesterday.
Sourie, as he was familiarly called from Sourfauld,
the name of his little farm, seemed, for some reason
or other, to have been appointed perpetual Brigadier-
General.

An old man then was Sourie, but still straight as
a ramrod, and approaching the heroic in height.
There were few opportunities for training orators in
Sillerton, but had there been, Sourie would certainly
have borne the bell.

I recollect some of the old man's quaint sayings,
and there was a very marked difference between
them and the utterances that came from his less
gifted neighbors. Perhaps, were I ever to visit the
churchyard of the old parish I might trace the
rudely-carved lines that tell where the farmer of

Sourfauld was gathered to his fathers, and not inappropriately repeat the line—

"Some mute, inglorious Milton here may rest."

It is with the live Sourie, however, that I am now dealing, and as he stands there at the head of the Gardeners of Sillerton. But what a wonderful metamorphosis has taken place, and who would recognize the plainly-clad and somewhat patched tenant of Sourfauld in the towering Goliath who directs the movements of the Gardeners?

The bearskin cap of a Life-Guardsman would have hid its diminished head before the lofty headpiece that Sourie wore. Who designed it, or why it was so designed, has not been written amongst the chronicles of Sillerton.

The Spartan warrior who fell in battle was borne home upon his shield. Was it possible that the Sillerton designer of martial garments knew something of ancient history, and moved by the careful thrift of his own countrymen, and profiting by the recollection of Spartan adaptation, so constructed the helmets of our local warriors that, should the wearer fall in battle, he might be easily and economically buried in his capacious headgear?

A bright scarlet coat, somewhat resembling what our fighting forefathers wore about a half-century

before, covered the greater part of the elongated form
of the commander-in-chief, and partly concealed a
pair of gigantic boots that resembled very much
those worn by swashbucklers in the time of Crom-
well, while a remarkably long sword completed the
outfit, so far at least as my memory warrants a
description.

Whence that sword came has often been a source
of wonder to my boyhood days. Could it have been
found near Wallace Neuk in the brave toon o' Bon-
Accord?

Might some local antiquary have lent it for the
occasion, or did the village blacksmith, in a moment
of high warlike spirit, design and fashion the terrible weapon that, like the helmet of Navarre,
blazed as a guiding star in front of the Gardeners,
who now, to the clang of martial music, tramped
around the village square, and four deep, marched
straight through the shady walks of the home park
to the House of Sillerton, the residence of the Hon-
orary Chief of the Gardeners, and where the commander-in-chief and his men went through a species
of royal salute? Poor Sourie! when I recall the old
man to my memory, I think of him as Oliver Wen-
dell Holmes thought of his so-called "Last Leaf":—

> "I know it is a sin
> For me to sit and grin

> At him here ;
> But the old three-cornered hat,
> And the breeches, and all that,
> Are so queer ! "

On the conclusion of these preliminary exercises, prizes were given for the best floral designs, slight refreshments were handed round, the patron's health was drunk in a bumper of good Scotch, three ringing cheers were given, and to the inspiring music of the brass band, whose whistles had now been duly moistened, the Ancient Gardeners wended their way back to the village.

Probably the gentle reader may here be ready to say, " We are done with the Gardeners now." Not by any means. The parade is over, flags and spears, and aprons, drums, fifes, and swords are laid aside, but the real business of the Gardeners of Sillerton is now only beginning.

I have heard it said, that after all, the Gardeners of Sillerton were incorporated simply to enjoy a dinner once a year in the roomy dining-room of the Gamut Arms. This may or may not be the case, but I certainly knew one individual who joined the society for this special object, and for no other. "Protty," as he was nicknamed, was one of the characters of the locality, and while usually leading a sober and industrious life, yet, on high occasions, got somewhat befuddled, and on the occasion of the Gardeners' dinner got gloriously fou.

Protty, like Lazarus of old, got few of the good things of this life, but he determined that at least once a year there should be an exception to the rule, and cheerfully paid his annual subscription to enjoy the coveted luxuries of the annual dinner.

And what a dinner was there! The season for haggis had not yet come, but haggis was quite a common dish in the locality, and did not exercise that influence upon the salivary glands that it does upon Scotchmen in foreign lands, who meet to enjoy that great national dish once a year, namely, on the natal day of Scotland's patron saint. But beef and greens were there; mighty rounds fit to set before a Queen; fish, fowl, and all the et-ceteras that in those days went to constitute a feast that was required by, and demanded too, a vigorous appetite. It was verily "strong meat for strong men."

But how much of these luxuries fell to the lot of poor Protty? The fact was that the wags of Siller-ton—and their name was "Legion"—knowing Protty's relish for good things, had so ordered it that not one of the luxuries should reach, in Protty's case, their legitimate destination. Protty was able, during the progress of the dinner, to enjoy the nips of whisky that followed, or perhaps accompanied, certain courses, but a dish of mashed turnips, heavily sweetened with sugar, and replenished again and again, was all that Protty was permitted to enjoy, Protty being too obfuscated by repeated libations to see the trick that was being played upon him.

Such was one of the standing, practical, and perennial jokes that were relished in those days, and doubtless very heartily laughed at by those who cheated the Ancient Gardener of his due.

That all this was very reprehensible who will deny, yet, personally, I feel no responsibility. I promised to paint Sillerton, not as it should have been, but simply as it was, and I doubt not there are some yet amongst the denizens of the parish, who, if they ever cast their eyes upon this page will remember well the stalwart frame and honest, homely speech of the leader of the Ancient Gardeners—Sourie of Sourfauld : and as they revive the story of the mashed turnips—the only dish partaken of by the fuddled Gardener—will not the phrase—the well-known, the oft-repeated phrase—be repeated again—" Protty ! Protty ! Sandy Mackie " ?

CHAPTER XVII.

THE WARS OF THE ROSES.

" Spare your comparisons," replied
  An angry Rose, who grew beside ;
" Of all mankind you should not flout us ;
  What can a poet do without us ?
  In every love-song roses bloom ;
  We lend you color and perfume."
            —JOHN GAY.

FEAR not, gentle reader ; the humble historian of
Sillerton's quiet ways has no intention of appro-
priating the pen of a Macaulay or a Napier, and
whisking you off to the great battlefields of Hindos-
tan or of Merrie England.

A theme more becoming an Aberdeenshire chron-
icler, were he martially inclined, might be found
nearer home, and doubtless he would find a suitable
subject for his talent in the " sair field o' Har-
law "—

  " When Donald came branking down the brae
    Wi' twenty thousand men."

Our " Wars of the Roses " were simply the
friendly competitions that took place at the annual
meeting of the Gardeners of Sillerton, between our

rival horticulturists, and where the rose, *par excel-lence*, played a very prominent part. Indeed, before dismissing the parade of the said Gardeners, if I have not already done so, I have one incident more to relate, without which my narrative, to me, at least, would seem incomplete.

I have already remarked the extraordinary interest that the Gardeners' Day excited both in village and district. The local amateur horticult-urists—and there were several such in the neighbor-hood, who, in addition to success in growing their favorites, possessed the art as well of arranging them in beautiful forms and combinations—had a peculiarly deep interest in the day.

Apart from the pleasure that success would bring, there was, in addition, the satisfaction that the money value of the prizes won would also afford. And thus there was a double stimulant supplied. Secretly each competitor formed his plans and carried them out. No State secret was more jeal-ously guarded than his, and no rival, or indeed any-body else, would be allowed to obtain the faintest glimpse of the mere skeleton that now, bare and uninteresting, would, on the great marshalling day of the Gardeners, stand in the Sillerton Square arrayed in all the beauty that a rainbow robe of exquisite flowers would lend.

Truly Solomon in all his glory was not arrayed like one of these. The interest also was of a double character, and that of the competitor was shared by all the boys of Sillerton.

We had each of us our favorite, and him we were pledged to aid and abet to the best of our ability. I fancy I hear one saying—"But in what way could aid be given?" Well, that is an easy matter to explain.

While the embryo floral crown, or whatever device it might be, was complete in every part—complete in so far as the mere skeleton or framework could be called complete—yet its flowery robes and adornments must needs be all added on the morning of the parade. And thus we became jackals to the lion. We arranged beforehand with non-competitors, who would, early on the morning of the eventful day, give us the gleanings, nay, the whole yield, of their gardens.

The friend who provided me with my floral tribute was known in the parish by the name of General Hay. Let me now introduce the old man. Upwards of six feet in height, at least fourscore years of age, yet unbent by time or infirmity, the General has anticipated our errand, and is already in his garden awaiting our arrival. He greets us kindly, and smiles as he marks the number of baskets we carry, for I had secured a partner in the carrying business, and the said baskets conveyed the gentlest of hints that our demands upon his flower-garden would not by any means be of a modest nature.

I believe, however, he took this as a compliment, and had he been possessed of the Oriental "Gardens of Gul," or been entitled to glean Mount Hybla's roses, he would have culled every flower, rather than send us away unsatisfied.

As to the old gentleman's habiliments, a pair of knee-breeches, with long tight stockings, and buckled shoes, as a continuation, finished his outfit as to the lower extremities, and showed a pair of long, thin legs that harmonized admirably with his "tout ensemble." The coat had a half military look, showing a very capacious and high collar, and extending nearly to his knees. The well-buttoned vest did not allow much of his breast linen to be seen, but this was more than equalized by a remarkably high shirt collar that rose above the ears. I never saw such another but once, when I made one of my first visits to Aberdeen. The amount of cloth around the individual's neck induced me to ask his name, and my companion informed me that the wags had named him the " British Linen Company."

But I seem to have forgotten the head-piece, and

left that to be last described which generally should claim first notice. "Cap-a-pied" with me seems to have been reversed, but I shall take the reader into my confidence and tell why I adopted that course. It may be possible that I was thinking of Robert Browning's Christmas Eve, and that personally I might be a twin brother, at least in spirit, of that

> Artist of another ambition,
> Who, having a block to carve, no bigger,
> Has spent his power on the opposite quest,
> And believed to begin at the feet was best,
> For so may I see, ere I die, the whole figure !—"

The fact was, however, that, like the small boy, I kept the sweetest morsel on the side of my plate for the last mouthful. The *bon bouche* was an excellent close to the feast. It was not exactly the Glengarry cap that attracted my attention, for the General in this respect resembled Rob Rorison—

> It wasna the bonnet, but the head that was in it,
> Made every one speak o' Rob Rorison's bonnet.

And so with General Hay—not the bonnet, but the head itself, attracted the attention. The last "queue" that was worn in Sillerton hung from that head. I had often seen the "queue" in pictures that represented a generation that had almost passed away, but on the living subject, with this one exception, never.

11

Why General Hay clung to this relic of a past age when all his contemporaries went "shaven and shorn," it were hard to say, and supplied a problem to the young antiquaries of the village that was never solved. But there it was, and in the church on Sunday, where its owner was always in his place, it attracted more attention, I fear, from the younger members of the congregation than the somewhat dry yet classic utterances of the staid and stately Robert Fordyce.

It was as well a matter of no small curiosity to me to know how Hay had received his "soubriquet" of General, and it at least proves the prevalence of that vein of fun and humor that existed in Sillerton, and which, so often, as we have seen, came to the surface. All the small boys associated old Hay with scenes of carnage and blood, and no doubt believed that he had played no unimportant part in the military history of the country. Personally, I was reluctantly undeceived, and learned from an old sergeant of artillery, whom I often visited to hear his account of battles in the Peninsula, in which he had taken a part, that the old man had never seen nor heard a shot fired in anger.

When the Scottish youth enrolled themselves members of the Militia that prepared to meet any threatened invasion, Hay found himself a full private in a company of which the junior lieutenant owned the same name as himself. To what particular branch of the family Lieutenant Hay belonged it would be difficult now to say, as the Hays were decidedly a fighting family; many of them rose to distinction in the army, and if Generals there were among them—and undoubtedly there were—will not their names and deeds be all duly recorded in the military annals of Aberdeenshire?

When the rumors of war and the smoke of battle cleared away, Private Hay converted his spear into a pruning-hook, and condescended to cultivate cabbages and roses in a quiet and cosy neuk not far from the gate of Paradise.

The warlike Lieutenant decided otherwise; buckled on his sword the more tightly, and went to fight his country's battles wherever and whenever fighting was required. Step by step Hay rose in rank in his profession of arms, until one day the news reached Sillerton that the whilom Lieutenant was now General Hay. For some reason or other, now unknown, and queer though the idea may seem, yet the good folks of Sillerton insisted, in an overflowing fit of fun and frolic, on raising their own peaceful Hay to the same rank with his more warlike namesake. In fact he became, in one sense, the military hero's "Double-ganger." The *soi-disant*

Lieutenant Hay of Sillerton became eventually, after passing through all the intermediate gradations of rank, General Hay, and General Hay he remained to the end.

He never resented the courtesy that gave him rank, and responded to his title as naturally as if he had won it on the field of battle. He was a kindly old man, and ever sent us—small boys— away infinitely pleased with our reception, and loaded with the beautiful treasures of his garden.

May his ashes rest in peace ! His memory to me is still as fragrant and fresh as the sweet-scented roses that he once grew.

The Sillertonians, though brimful of fun, yet invariably left it behind them when they visited the resting-places of the dead, and yet, incongruous as it may seem, I often wonder if they carved the name "General" on his tombstone in the churchyard of Sillerton.

Having begun this chapter with unmeasured eulogies of the rose, I fear that the unwarlike General Hay led me away from my first love, and that the peculiar circumstances that gave him his tinsel rank, and the charms of a peaceful life, that made him supremely happy amongst his flowers, made me almost forget the prominent part that the rose, whether red or white, or damask, played in the Gardeners' ompetition in Sillerton.

I shall at once acknowledge the guilt, and make the only reparation in my power, by closing this portion of my reminiscences in the following, though very slightly altered, lines of the immortal Keats :—

I saw the sweetest flower wild nature yields—
  A fresh-blown musk rose ; 'twas the first that threw
  Its sweets upon the summer ; graceful it grew
As is the wand that Queen Titania wields.
And as I feasted on its fragrancy
  I thought the garden-rose it far excell'd ;
But when, oh, Hay ! thy roses came to me,
  My sense with their deliciousness was spell'd :
Soft voices had they, that with tender plea,
  Whisper'd of peace, and truth, and friendliness
    unquell'd.

CHAPTER XVIII.

PRACTICAL JOKERS AT WORK.

Take thy beak from out my heart, and take thy form from
    off my door.
            Quoth the raven, "Nevermore."

                                                POE.

WHILE not going quite so far as the Aberdonian
who is reported by Max O'Rell as saying, "Tak
awa Aberdeen and a few miles roun' aboot it, and
whar are ye?" I yet cannot forget that in the shire,
at least, of Aberdeen there was a vast amount of
that species of wit in my boyhood days that found
a ready outlet in practical jokes, as I have had occasion frequently to note in this picture of Sillerton
life that I have been attempting not to paint but to
reproduce.

Protty Sandy Mackie was not the only victim that
was bagged by the Sillerton jokers, but I shall con-
trive to give one or two instances that came under
my personal observation, and which I shall attempt
as well to narrate within reasonable limits.

That the village store, or shop as it was then

called, should be a common rendezvous on a Saturday evening goes without saying, and there, accordingly, both buyers and sellers convened; stories were there told, and there practical jokes were sometimes perpetrated that, as we shall see, occasionally left indelible marks behind them.

The shopkeeper, or merchant, as he was designated in those days, was a man of considerable energy in his calling, and did not confine his attention altogether to the ordinary style of doing business. In fact, the merchant came of an enterprising family, and showed it in more than one way, as his transactions proved. One Saturday evening, when the store was pretty full of customers—served and to be served—Mr. Baggs informed them that he had made a fortunate venture in the way of foot-gear, and in consequence was prepared to sell boots at a price that would strike dumb the souters of Sillerton. The goods were there and then produced, and so well did they look, that sales to a considerable extent were at once effected.

A near relative of mine was there, but he had made no purchases. Being asked if he would not invest in a pair of boots, he stated that he would rather deal in a different way. He said in fact, that he would much prefer to take his boots by the year, or, in other words, that Mr. Baggs should take a twelve months' contract, and keep him in foot-gear during that time for a certain amount, the said amount to be then and there agreed on between them.

This proposition being somewhat novel, was received with great applause by the crowd generally, and was at once favorably entertained by the merchant, whose heart was considerably opened by the number of sales he had effected that evening and the profits realized.

The sum was, after a little haggling, settled; the terms were agreed to, and a note was at once drawn up defining the terms of the agreement, signed and duly witnessed. I remember quite well one or two of the conditions. One was that a boot might, if it required such repairs, be only twice soled and, after the second soling to become the property of the wearer. Another was that no patch whatever was to be placed on the uppers, but that, when such an operation became necessary, the dilapidated boots were to be returned to the merchant and replaced by a new pair.

There was much merriment over the novel contract, but as the price to be paid seemed large for a twelvemonths' wear of boots, the laugh was clearly on the merchant's side. How the laugh turned to another quarter we shall presently see.

My friend was employed in the Garioch district at a considerable distance from Sillerton; he returned home every Saturday evening, and I usually went with my pony to meet him the greater part of the way, when we contrived to get home by the well-known process of "Ride and Tie." I now, however, got instructions to no longer make my usual Saturday trip, as my friend intended walking until his boot contract was finished.

The first Saturday night came, and with it came Dick, as I may call my relative, who, after supper, speedily found his way to the village store to have his boots examined. They were pronounced sea-worthy by the referee, but there were deep traces of tear and wear that went to Mr. Baggs' heart. It was evident that another trip beyond Bennachie and back, with nearly a week's work thrown in, would change considerably the rating of Dick's boots. The "A 1." would certainly go down the scale.

Another Saturday night came, and Dick and his boots came also. The weather had been bad; the distance to be traversed was long; the roads were execrable, and the fears of the shopkeeper were fully realized, for two new soles had to be ordered from the village cobbler, while Dick marched off in triumph with his feet snugly encased in another pair of Mr. Baggs' boots.

It is needless to say that this process went on much in the same way till the end of the twelve months. The story meantime had got wind, and every youngster who could find an excuse for purchasing the smallest article contrived to be in the village store just about the hour when Dick generally put in an appearance, and almost invariably with a pair of dilapidated boots.

Everybody enjoyed the chagrin of poor Baggs, who was the butt of the parish for a twelvemonth and more, and no happier man was there in Sillerton than he when the boot contract was eventually and finally closed. Curiosity tried hard to worm out of Baggs the exact state of his account in this boot transaction, but the village shopkeeper declined to respond ; silent was Baggs as a very oyster ; he preferred to keep his own secret, and the village book-keepers succeeded in arriving only at an approximation.

It was well known, however, that the balance was on the wrong side of " Profit and Loss, " at least so far as Baggs was concerned. Probably a Yankee might have guessed that the boot was on the wrong leg. The only one that had reason to regret the closing of the boot-contract was my pony Donald.

When Baggs' boots ceased to be worn on contract, Donald's services were on demand once more, and Saturday afternoons now found him no longer enjoying his ease in his cosy stall, but on a return trip from the back of Bennachie, and alternately carrying on his back his light-weight master, and a somewhat sturdier rider, who no longer wore boots supplied by contract, and who now enjoyed a "lift" on his Saturday trip homeward. After all Baggs was only a little in advance of his age, and was a true type of those who sell everything, from a "needle to an anchor," and who would feel ashamed were they unable to supply on demand an umbrella or a sentry box.

> " He had a fouth o' auld nick-nackets,
>   Rusty airn caps and jinglin' jackets,
>   Wad haud the Lothians three in tackets,
>   A towmont guid,
>   And parritch-pats and auld saut-backets :
>   Before the Flood."

CHAPTER XIX.

THE WINNING LEG.

Ae market night
Tam had got planted unco right ;
Fast by an ingle bleezin' finely,
Wi' reaming swats that drank divinely,
                    Tam o' Shanter.

HAD I the intention of being mysterious, I could
scarcely have adopted a better heading to this
chapter than I have done.   The winning card might
be easily understood, even in the quiet village of
Sillerton, where a friendly rubber was played by the
upper ten in the manse parlor or in the gentleman-
farmer's drawing-room, and where "catch-the-ten"
was the favorite game amongst the lads and lasses
of the parish, with a touch "of old maid" now and
then indulged in, just to vary the entertainment.

The winning horse might also be understood,
when farmer bodies, with sharper spurs in their
heads than on their heels, occasionally tried the
mettle of their nags.

But the winning leg was out of the ordinary run
of the village vocabulary, and would have puzzled

a Sillertonian as much as a quadratic equation would
have done a celebrated Aberdeen professor, who
never got past the golden rule of three, but whose
fervid eloquence has roused Scotchmen to enthusi-
asm from John O'Groats to wherever Scotchmen
are known, and that means the "warl' ower."

Well, it will be in order now to explain, but I
claim the privilege ot telling my story in my own
way. As was said in a previous chapter, the Inverurie markets, which I think were of monthly occurrence, were a source of pleasure and profit to the
business folks of Sillerton, and groups of these,
mounted on their bob-tailed nags (for the blood
horse had scarcely yet become a favorite amongst
our rugged hill roads, and the gig or phaeton was
put into requisition only when ladies were in the
case), were to be seen trotting along quietly and
doucely towards the ancient burgh.

I would not say that the pace homeward in the
evening was quite so quiet and formal, but this
might be easily accounted for by the fact known to
every naturalist, that the horse on the home-stretch
is a much fleeter animal than when his head is turned
away from his own oat-bin.

The Rev. Sydney Smith, of happy memory, who
lived for years in Edinburgh, where there were literary giants in those days, and who yet gravely

asserted that it would require a surgical operation to get a joke into a Scotchman's head, was a close observer of human nature, as we may judge by the above assertion, and carried his observations also into that of the equine family.

Sydney was well aware of this propensity of the horse to hasten towards his own oat-bin, and so ordered it that, in the case of a horse he possessed, the oat-bin should be ever before him. "Calamity" had defied all efforts of whip or spur to accelerate his movements, and Smith at last hit upon the happy expedient of fastening a small vessel containing a feed of oats upon the end of an elongated shaft. This worked as a veritable charm, and the witty parson was borne along at a rattling speed, while the very sight of the golden grain before his eyes stimulated the craving steed to redouble his efforts to overtake every moment what he eventually reached only when he got home.

It may be at the same time quite possible that what added to Tam o' Shanter's courage, may have helped the Sillerton farmers to shorten, at least by time, the trip homewards from the Inverurie monthly market. In fact, it was pretty widely known that farmers generally returned home from these markets pretty well corned, as the saying was.

Nor was it looked upon as in any way strange

that such should be. Opinion, indeed, leant exactly in the other way. I once heard a very peculiar exemplification of this. A well-to-do farmer was boasting that he at least had never come home from a market in that happy and exhilarated state. His wife, a lady of the highest culture, and certainly one of the leaders of fashion in the parish, but withal possessed of a considerable amount of homely Scotch humor, very naively replied to her husband's boast, " Well, George, and if you did sometimes, I would not think a bit the less of you." Did it follow that she would have thought the more?

I often joined the cavalcade as a matter, not of business, but of pleasure, and if I did not learn much about the price and quality of different sorts of grain, nor of those agricultural questions that were often keenly discussed, even in the saddle, I yet gleaned some knowledge of human nature, that may have sometimes helped me in after-life.

On our arrival the horses were usually stabled at a well-known hostelry within the burgh, and there, towards evening, when all market business was at an end, the riders met to enjoy the stirrup-cup before mounting their nags for the homeward ride. Maybe strict veracity might suggest that cup should be used in the plural number, as there were occasions when Tom Ledingham's blend rendered it somewhat difficult to leave the table just at the end of the first tumbler. Stories, too, did not always quite fit the emptying of the glasses, and the equalizing of the two things often cost time and money both, when an "eke" had to be taken to get ends to meet.

One evening matters were precisely in this state, and a Sillerton farmer, to twit mine host of the Elphinstone Arms, would persist in telling funny things about Inverurie, and, amongst others, a story of one of the local clergy who had preached lately in the neighboring church, very soon after the close of a keenly-contested election of bailies and other officials for the burgh.

Things had not gone precisely in accordance with the minister's political views, and probably he would have preferred to take no notice whatever of the magistracy that now sat very conspicuously before him. The custom, however, was, in the closing prayer, to pray for those in authority over us, and custom in the Auld Kirk was like a law of the Medes and Persians, "it altered not." The minister duly conformed to the custom, and pray he did, but in a way that doubtless failed to excite the admiration of the subjects of his supplications, "God bless the Magistrates o' this ancient burgh, sic as they are."

One roar of laughter from the Sillertonians greeted this anecdote, and mine host had to own that the tale had been truthfully told. One story led to another, one of which referred to feats of strength that the narrator had witnessed, and this probably tempted the landlord, who was a man of ponderous dimensions, to wager a bottle of hot Scotch, that his leg would measure, round the calf, more than that of any man in the company. At first no one seemed inclined to take up the challenge, but at length a farmer who lived near us, and who was certainly the smallest man in the room, called out, "Tam, I'll tak' your bet, man."

Sim Eddie was our neighbor, and I quietly attempted to dissuade him from his rash offer, but to no purpose. He was resolute, and I was appointed judge or umpire. The landlord's leg was produced and duly taped, and from appearances no one doubted but that little Sim would have to foot the bill, for no one thought that he could possibly leg it. Nothing daunted, Sim in turn presented his leg for measurement, but, ye gods! what a leg was there!

We were all amazed, and any measurement seemed unnecessary, but yet the tape had to do its duty, and Eddie's leg took two inches of the line more than Tom's. This settled the matter, and the bottle of hot Scotch was a free stirrup-cup to the farmers of Sillerton.

12

As we rode homeward I could not help wondering how it was possible that so small a man should have so large a leg, and, sidling up to the winner of the bet, I plumped the question, "How does it happen, Sim, that you have so big a leg?" The honest farmer answered me at once, "Weel, laddie, I'll jist tell you. Ye'll recollect I had ance the scarlet fivver, an' got a' richt again; bit the dregs o't settled in that leg. That's jist it; bit eh, man, wasna I frichtened that I wad hae to exhibit the ither ane, for as sure's death it's a perfect spindleshank!"

The reader may readily conceive the merriment that rose at the explanation. But the joke did not end here exactly. It oozed out over the whole countryside, for Ledingham was well known throughout the bounds of the Garioch, and the badgering he got over that leg-wager was enough to kill any ordinary man.

It worked, however, in a different way with the host of the Elphinstone Arms. In fact, Ledingham nearly killed two commercial travellers who had carried their quizzing rather far, and after some time it came to be understood generally, and particularly amongst the farmers of Sillerton, that, in the matter of the "Winning Leg," silence was golden, and would undoubtedly prove a winning card, at least in one of the hotels in the neighborhood of Inverurie.

CHAPTER XX.

THE MINISTER'S CHRISTMAS DINNER.

And now farewell each dainty dish,
  With sundry sorts of sugared wine !
Farewell, I say, fine flesh and fish,
  To please this dainty mouth of mine !
I now, alas, must leave all these,
And make good cheer with bread and cheese !
  —BRETON.

THE Rev. Robert Fordyce, minister of Sillerton,
was a douce, sober man in every way—the last man
in the world to poke fun at anybody, and the very
last, certainly, who should have been the victim of
a practical joke. The festive season was now approaching, and his reverence had been duly invited
to eat his sixtieth Christmas dinner at the hospitable table of a parishioner, the tenant of Milton.

Invitations in those days did not contain the
cabalistic letters, "R.S.V.P.," but yet the Reverend
Robert had forwarded his acceptance, and had every
intention of honoring the entertainment with his
presence.

The guidwife of Milton soared somewhat above
the ordinary run of farmers' wives. She had seen

a little of the world beyond the boundary line of
Sillerton, and she dearly loved, on occasion, to see
a choice company enjoying themselves round her
groaning mahogany. And so the minister and a
few other favored ones were invited to eat their
Christmas dinner at Milton.

But here it behoves us to introduce another character upon the scene. No minister was ever complete without his man, and even the Scriptural
fox-tail story could scarcely have been told, without
a minister to preach, and a minister's man to whistle.
Gentle reader, allow me to introduce to you John
Sprot, the minister's man. John, indeed, was no
ordinary man.

From boyhood he had served the clergy, and if
not yet arrived at the years of discretion, certainly
from the influence of precept and example he should
have reached that goal long ago.

John had, in fact, become manse and glebe property, and in that capacity had described a circle, a
sort of ecclesiastical circle, throughout the bounds
of the Presbytery, until he now found himself general manager for Mr. Fordyce of Sillerton, delving
in the manse garden, cultivating the glebe generally,
and when his master, who was no Jehu, held his
annual "catechizing" throughout the parish, or
once on a while accepted an invitation to dinner,

driving him in the old gig that had now for more than a quarter of a century been the admiration of the little boys of Sillerton.

But just here the question naturally arises—Why had not Sprot settled down in one favored spot? Why was John still a rolling stone that gathers no moss? Well, there is a delicacy in the answer that the writer of this humble narrative feels keenly, but yet the truth, the sober truth, must be told. John Sprot was, in fact, a ——. No, I don't exactly mean that, but while John was a strong advocate of temperance, yet the flesh was sometimes weak, and so it happened that, on a few occasions, John had been what Scotch folks kindly call "overtaken."

The consequence of this was that when his reverence then weighed his man in the scales of sobriety, and found him wanting, pastures new had to be looked for, and another manse door closed behind him forever.

During, however, one of John's escapades, an accident had converted one of his seemly legs into something resembling an arc of a circle, and while this gave him a most peculiar style of perambulation, even in his soberest seasons, yet it was generally believed that good would come of it, and that his conduct in the future would be as straight as his lower member was crooked.

A whole year, last Martinmas, had come and gone, and John Sprot was still the minister's man of Sillerton. If temptation had come, it had evidently also been successfully resisted, and the more observant of the villagers had begun to express an opinion, that John might close his earthly career in the cosy manse of Sillerton. Alas! how weak is human nature at best—but no, we must not anticipate.

The day of Milton's dinner-party came, and, if great preparations were made by the guidwife of Milton, the minister's man was far from idle. Under the genial influence of soap-suds and an abundant supply of elbow-grease, the ancient gig had actually renewed its age, and the old gray, through the persuasive action of a new curry-comb, had parted with a few pounds of that fur which, if it increased warmth, at the same time very materially diminished speed. John felt somewhat exhausted with his unwonted exertions, but experienced a keen satisfaction in the reflection that man, horse, and gig were ready for action.

Seating himself upon an old wheelbarrow that stood invitingly near, he contemplated with considerable satisfaction his work, and, as he lighted his pipe, and began to feel the influence of the subtle narcotic, he felt supremely happy, and it is at least doubtful, had the change been possible, if at that moment he would have exchanged places with the Reverend Robert Fordyce of Sillerton.

Just then a small callant that ran messages about the village appeared on the scene, and intimated to John, that Marshal Graham, now manager of the Sillerton distillery, requested to see him with the least possible delay. Graham was a confirmed practical joker, and seldom did a week pass without some new cantrip on his part that set the whole country side roaring with laughter.

Sprot, impressed with the seeming importance of the message, hesitated not for a moment, but at once proceeded to the office, where he was received with marked courtesy. Graham informed him with the utmost gravity that last night he had been grossly insulted by the land steward, James Power, and, knowing John's character for probity and caution, he requested him to carry to Power a note demanding an immediate apology, failing which he said he believed the matter would end in bloodshed.

John was considerably dumfounded by this startling intelligence, but a sense of the confidence placed in him, along with a horn of Sillerton's best dew, nerved him for his delicate mission, and away he went to deliver the somewhat hostile note. Having read the threatening message, Power pretended to get

into a terrible passion, tearing the letter in pieces
and swearing that blood alone could settle the dis-
pute between them.   A reply was instantly penned,
and, charged with another horn of the same generous
sedative that he had swallowed only a few minutes
before, John soon placed Power's note in Graham's
hands.

The fact was, that the two worthies, knowing that
the minister was due that evening at Milton, con-
ceived the brilliant idea of putting John Sprot *hors
de combat*, and so spoil the parson's dinner, seeing
that it was an established fact that the old gentleman could no more drive a horse and buggy, than he
could have directed the manœuvres of an ironclad.

Back and forth went Sprot; letter after letter was
written by the two belligerents, horn followed horn
with the now decidedly obfuscated minister's man,
until Milton's Christmas dinner had passed from his
memory like a flitting dream.   The barley bree that
makes some men pugnacious, only softened the
tenderest sensibilities of John's heart.

He fancied that he was engaged in the noble work
of pouring oil on troubled waters; without his individual efforts, human blood might have been shed,
and, feeling thus, we fear the malt got aboon the
meal ; the heartless jokers were only too successful,
and the apostle of peace fell before the syren bland-

ishments of Sillerton's ripest—mellowest—purest mountain dew.

But where was the Reverend Robert Fordyce all this time? He had seen the earlier exertions of his faithful servant; he had watched from the manse windows the marked progress of John's work; the old gray looked as if the vagaries of colthood might be again assumed; the antiquated gig reminded the douce parson that correct truly was Keats when he penned the line:—

" A thing of beauty is a joy for ever,"

and dreaming of no malign influence to cross his path, he resigns himself to pleasing waking dreams of many a merry Christmas that he had seen and kept, before the manse was still and lonely as now; when childish voices and pattering feet were wont to reach unchallenged his own quiet snuggery, and before he had known what it was to read a portion of one's own history on the mossgrown stone that he could even now see from the study window.

But dreaming will scarcely clothe the minister of Sillerton for his Christmas dinner. And so he bestirs himself anew. The decent broadcloth becomes his rounded figure well; the shirt front, heavily ruffled, looks like the driven snow; a chain, resplendent with keys and seals, passes to and forth across his breast;

and with feet encased in warm overshoes, and closely buttoned in a ponderous overcoat that two maiden daughters arrange lovingly around him, the Reverend Mr. Fordyce smiles kindly upon his surroundings, and, passing through his hall to the gravelled walk in front, takes his first step in the direction of his Christmas dinner.

But where was John Sprot now? Where the renovated gig? Where the rejuvenated gray? The minister peers curiously towards the manse stables. He sees something approaching, but not precisely what he expected. The horse and gig were just as they should be, but, alas! John Sprot, the minister's man, was where no minister's man should be, at least when under orders to drive his master to a Christmas dinner.

John had been placed, by officious hands doubtless, upon the back of the gallant gray, but there was assuredly a bar-sinister in his surroundings—his face was towards the tail, and two callants, who had evidently been engaged for the occasion, were trying as best they could, to enable the driver to preserve his equilibrium, and to direct at the same time the movements of the astonished gray towards the manse door.

One glance at the strange procession was enough for the minister, who quickly sought and found again the privacy of his own chamber; the now irate maidens divested him of his more outside coverings; the immaculate black was speedily exchanged for less pretentious garments; and instead of the savory turkey and ham, with all the et-ceteras that filled and adorned, that evening, the groaning table of the tenant of Milton, our douce minister was perforce content to dine on a cold joint that had done duty on the manse table the day before.

How the gig, the gray, and John Sprot (we here, for conscientious reasons, reverse the order of precedence) found their due and allotted places I know not. I do know that John awoke the day after Christmas "a sadder but a wiser man." This, however, was a season of mutual forbearance; forgiveness was asked and found; the merry wags were inclined to own that they had carried the joke a little too far; and in after-years, when the Reverend Robert Fordyce dispensed, on special and favored occasions, the blessings that covered his own table, he sometimes condescended to tell the story, with a slightly sad and pensive smile, how it happened that he missed his Milton dinner, on that now long-past Christmas day.

I need hardly say that Sprot's escapade was not so quickly forgotten by the jovial Sillertonians, as it was forgiven by the kindly minister, and the jokes

that were cracked on the occasion, and the excruci-
ating quizzing to which John was subjected, could
scarcely be borne by the victim with genuine
equanimity.

The fact also that it occurred at a time when con-
vivialities were in order, drew more attention to it
than had it happened at a busier season, and often
at bachelor dinners, long after, have I heard a song
sung, recounting John's Yuletime adventure, that
local talent had both composed and set to music.

There were three stanzas of this song, two of
which my memory had faithfully retained ; one had
irrevocably, at least so far as I was concerned, passed
away.   An esteemed correspondent, however, living
near the locality, and who, when very slightly
prompted, recollected all the circumstances of the
case, sent me the missing verse—strange to say,
the only one he could call to mind.   I am thus able
to supply the three verses, which, perhaps, are
curious enough to prove of interest to individuals
fond of "folk-lore."

The music I am unable to give; I believe it was
as original as the song.   The loss of this, at the same
time, is less to be regretted as the poetic effusion is
not likely to occupy a place on the programmes of
many "musical entertainments."

I give the song, chorus, etc., as I heard them of

old, only eliminating a few words that were slightly harsher than modern taste is now inclined to employ :—

JOHN SPROT.

> Great Johnny Sprot, the parson's man's
>   A man o' muckle pith,
> Wi' his fall, lall, derattle, tall,
>   Fall, lall, deday !
> Gin ye except the crookit leg,
>   He's soun' in limb an' lith,
> Wi' his fall, lall, derattle, tall,
>   Fall, lall, deday !
>
> As Johnny Sprot gaed o'er the burn,
>   He trampit on a snail,
> Wi' his fall, lall, derattle, tall,
>   Fall, lall, deday !
> Then up got Johnny's crookit leg,
>   An' in the burn he fell,
> Wi' his fall, lall, derattle tall,
>   Fall, lall, deday !
>
> The minister cam' stappin, oot,
>   Says, " John, far are ye, man ?
> Wi' yer fall, lall, derattle, tall,
>   Fall, lall, deday ! "
> Says John, " I've trampit on a snail,
>   An' d—— me bit I've faan,
> Wi' my fall, lall, derattle, tall,
>   Fall, lall, deday ! "

CHAPTER XXI.

SILLERTON'S BURDENS.

Go, therefore, now, and work ; for there shall no straw
be given you, yet shall ye deliver the tale of bricks.
The Israelites in Egypt.

I RECOLLECT distinctly an old friend of mine illus-
trating well the remark that we have all, in some
respect or other, something to trouble us.

Two elders of the kirk were engaged in a friendly
controversy, one urging that we all have some
trouble, the other as stoutly insisting that some
seemed to have no care whatever. During the discussion of the knotty question, which occurred as
they walked along the road, a well-known "feel "—
Jamie—hove in sight.

" Now," said the one elder, "I am ready to wager
that Jamie has no trouble in this world whatever."
The other as doggedly disbelieved this, and mean-
while the "feel" drew near. "Noo," says he who
believed in Jamie's perfect happiness, "hae ye ony-
thing to trouble ye, Jamie ?" "Fint a thing," quoth
Jamie, and was passing on. "Bide a wee," says the

other; "is there naething ava, Jamie, that bothers ye?" "Weel," replies the "feel," "John Tamson's bubbly jock leads me sometimes a sair time o't fin I'm gaen up the road." "Ah!" said the believer in universal sorrow, "ye see everybody has his 'bubbly-jock.'"

Gentle reader, this axiom or postulate was true also of Sillerton, for Sillerton undoubtedly had its "bubbly jock." I do not here refer so much to the village, in this case, but rather to the farmers of the parish. It was true that the villagers had found no royal road to affluence, nor did they expect to find it. They earned little, but their wants were in proportion to their means, and many of them, no doubt, felt like a celebrated New York divine, who, Socrates-like, was accustomed to stand periodically before one of the magnificently-filled windows of Broadway, and fervently thank the Lord that there were so many things in that window that he could do without.

Now the plain folks of Sillerton felt like the parson, without requiring to see the window. Certainly, in their case, where ignorance was bliss 'twere folly to be wise, and they were ignorant at least of greater wants, and hence were contented.

But amongst the farming community there was a slightly altered state of things. The common laborer scarcely hoped to lay past more than the merest trifle for a rainy day. The farmer aspired to something higher. He employed capital in his efforts to live, and he expected, not only to be able to pay his half-yearly rent, but also to have something besides on the right side of the "profit and loss" account. Nor was the farmer, on many of the larger estates, disappointed in his expectations.

It is related that Lord Aberdeen (the Premier Earl, I mean), when he met Her Majesty on her way to visit him at Haddo House, was accompanied by about four hundred horsemen. The Queen inquired who they were, and was informed that they were a portion of his tenantry. Expressing surprise that farmers could be so well mounted, his lordship explained that he would be ashamed to have a tenant on his estate who could not afford to keep as good a horse as he owned himself.

On the Richmond and Gordon property also a like liberal policy prevailed, and indeed on many or most of the large estates; but on smaller properties things were managed in a different way, and if there were wanting the Irish "middleman," yet the small Scotch laird extracted from his almost helpless tenant a considerably larger "tale of bricks" than that to which he was, in right and justice, entitled; and hence the anxiety and care and actual suffering that were so often the farmer's lot, and

which were the natural consequences of that iniqui-
tous system of "rack-rent" that, alas! was so
prevalent.

In Sillerton, successful farming was difficult of
realization. Rents were confessedly high—perhaps
a little too high—but the so-called Game Laws were
the veritable "bubbly-jock" of the parish. No
farmer on the estate, or in the parish, which in this
case were synonymous terms, had the right to keep
even a collie dog; no farmer was allowed to use a
gun over his farm; and no farmer might trap or kill
a hare or even rabbit, under any circumstances whatever—no, not in his own kail-yard.

Nor was this merely a negative condition, for by
the terms and conditions of his lease, he was bound
to protect these, and woe to him who failed to fulfil
his duty in this respect.

Were I imbued with the genius of a Mark Twain
or an Artemus Ward I might pause here simply to
moralize, and prove that the good Laird of Sillerton
was acting only in a true Christian spirit, and that
his leases, small codicils to the Gospels, made his
tenants better Christians, in that they were not only
admonished, but even compelled, to love their enemies the rabbits, and to do good to even the lower
animals that never ceased, night or day, to eat them
out, root, stock, and branch.

13

Personal tastes also may have influenced the leases, for the Laird was an ardent lover of game : he did not enjoy wandering for hours over his preserves without firing a shot, and he had as little wish to see his invited guests subjected to a like trying experience.

The expression "invited guests " leads me to note the fact, that, so far as parishioners were concerned, no one, no matter his education or social status, was ever invited to cast a fly upon the rippling waters of the "Bonnie Don," to try his luck with a fresh-run salmo salar, nor had he ever the chance to bag a snipe or moorfowl in the company of the Laird and his guests, the latter of whom came generally from England to spend a short holiday among the heather, or who belonged to the more aristocratic families of the district.

A few boys about the village plied their trouting rods over one or two mill-dams in the neighborhood, and were never challenged for doing so, but had we ventured a cast on the Don, we should have soon come to grief at the hands of the game-keepers.

We also contrived to make respectable baskets occasionally by a process we called "knittlin' "—probably the boys call it "tickling" now. We lay down on our faces close to a narrow stream, spreading out our arms to their utmost stretch, and while drawing them together, below the bank, we felt gently for trout, until our fingers creeping headwards, reached the gills. This point reached, they closed like a vice upon the victim, and the finny beauty was transferred to the creel.

This was a small privilege that the Laird allowed us, and yet it was of considerable value afterwards to the boys who enjoyed it. We manufactured our own rods; we constructed our own reels—"pirns" we called them then; we wove our own hair lines; and with a peculiar knot, deftly tied, we made our own casting lines. Nay, more, we prepared our own flies.

To the skill we acquired in doing these things I have often been indebted when some dire mishap broke in pieces our "tackle" on some lone Canadian lake, where many miles of weary portage-road separated us from skilled labor, or when the coquettish trout refused to be lured by a fly that had changed from bright scarlet to deep blue, until the exasperated angler began to assume the color of his own spurious fly.

On such occasions an hour of work—handicraft, I should say—learned on the banks of the Clyon-dam, made rods, reels, or lines as good as new, while a few tufts of the feathers of the scarlet Ibis, replacing the dismal blues, soon changed the aspect of affairs;

the fisher's sun of Austerlitz shone out once more; the sweet music of the reels began to ring again in our ears, and the speckled beauties of lake or stream quickly exchanged their native element for the shady corner that had been prepared for them in our birch-bark canoes.

It may not be out of place also to own, that while neither the village nor the parish sportsmen were invited to join the battue which, at the proper season, was held on our hills, and amongst our tree-covered and bushy "heughs and hows," yet the youths of the village had a way of obtaining sport, without any invitation whatever.

When we wanted a white or black rabbit—and such were occasionally seen in the warrens—we seldom failed to find what we wanted; and with a couple of boys on each side of a "dry-stane dyke," with eyes as keen as a pointer's nose, we generally succeeded in carrying home a few trophies of the chase. We conducted our operations in rabbit-hunting, however, on the still principle; we co-operated together, not by words, but by signs, and we never reached our homes until our distended jackets would no longer, in the growing darkness, be likely to attract attention, while the few stones that we had displaced in securing our game were more likely to be charged to the ruthless hand of time, than to any action that might be deemed an infraction of the Game Laws.

Some owners of game lands were not so conservative as he of Sillerton, and occasionally gave their tenantry, or at least a number of them, an opportunity of trying their skill with the hares, rabbits, and moor-fowl. This was considered a great compliment, and was heartily enjoyed by the participants in the sport.

I am compelled to own, also, that I have known invitations issued, I do not mean in Sillerton, not exactly to afford the tenantry a day's pleasant outing, but to give the gamekeepers an opportunity of marking individuals who, through skill in using the gun, and other "wrinkles" that indicate the sportsman, might be considered dangerous to game preserves, and who, in consequence, might be judiciously shadowed. For the correctness of this statement, I shall relate a short anecdote in illustration.

One autumn I was spending a few holidays with a well-to-do farmer, not far from the Vale of Alford. There was a prearranged meeting of the Chess Club of the district on hand, and we played chess for about three days; I might be nearer the truth by saying three days and nights. At last I struck work at the chess board, and told my host that there was no more chess for me for the next week. I said this, I believe, as if I meant it. " Weel," said my accommodating friend, " try the gun insteed. I hae the richt frae the laird to sheet ower the haill fairm." I looked surprised that he should have the privilege of shooting over his farm, which, along with a hundred acres or so of good arable land, included within its boundary-line a very large expanse of hill land, where he fed a few hundred sheep.

My expressed surprise was satisfied with the following explanation, which I shall repeat in his own words, if possible:—" Ye see, oor laird disna aften tribble his estates wi' his presence, bit, aboot twa years sinsyne, he cam' doon frae Lunnun, an' efter an ook's leesure, he sen's oot invitashuns to ilk ane o' his tenants for a day's sheetin'. My neebor Whitie an' mysell gat invitashuns like the lave, bit we jaloosed that there wis something in the thing that we didna jist clearly unerstan', and sae we keepit at hame. Weel, the upshot wis that the keepers, cannie chiels, pat their keel on a' the loons that were gey skeelie wi' the gun, while Whitie an' I gat permits to sheet whenever we liked."

I need scarcely say that I gladly availed myself of Newkeig's " permit," and, in consequence, made a few good bags along the heathery sides of the great Grampian range.

The jealous care exercised by the Laird of Siller-

ton over the preservation of his game, and the unlimited means at his disposal of increasing their
numbers indefinitely, could end only in one result.
That which happened in Australia in later years
with imported rabbits, which multiplied to such an
extent as to jeopardize the crops of those portions of
the Colony where they had been placed, happened
long before in Sillerton.

The red deer could occasionally be seen browsing
amongst the grain and turnips; the beautiful and
fleet roe might, every hour of the day, gladden the
heart of a Landseer had he decided to extend his
professional rambles to the parish of Sillerton; and
hares and rabbits, moor-fowl and black-cock fed,
and sported, and crowed as if the better part of the
parish were their own. And so it was.

Forty or fifty hares were often to be seen at one
time, and on one turnip-field; the grouse came in
clouds to claim their share of the harvest; the deer
were almost as tame as sheep, as they browsed on
the richest pastures of the farm; and, to crown all,
flocks of pheasants, housed, tended, and fed and
pampered with assiduous care, often left a field of
grain almost as worthless as if a hurricane had
swept over it. And he who, by every right under
heaven, owned those pastures, who sowed them, and
who should have reaped those fields, would have as

soon thought of joining a Guy Fawkes in a new
Gunpowder Plot, as of firing off a blunderbuss,
or even a pengun, to drive the voracious harpies
away.

It is true that the Laird and his friends made, at
the proper season of the year, heavy bags on the
fields and moors; it is true that a few bucks occasionally bit the dust before the unerring tube; it is
true that as many as thirty thousand rabbits had
been trapped or shot in the parish during one year,
and yet there was no appreciable relief to the poor
game-eaten farmer.

One tenant alone, a gentleman born and bred,
resisted the good Laird, and attempted to protect
his crops from the ravages of the rabbits. Alas! in
vain. His farm was intersected by belts of wood-
land, amongst which to enter, to follow up his de-
stroyers, would be counted a trespass and punish-
able by a fine; detectives were placed to mark if the
obnoxious tenant overstepped the limits of his own
farm, and, after a time, a conviction of hopelessness
came over him, and his futile attempts at self-preservation ceased.

His lease came, a year or two after, to a close, and
the farm was no longer for him; the gentleman
farmer did not thrive under the Upas shadow of the
Laird of Sillerton; a fitter and more plastic ten-

ant was found in a mannie that wore a Kilmarnock
bonnet on Sunday, and who, it was understood, had
made affidavit that he had never fired a gun in his
life.

In consequence of damage received, and for which
no compensation could be recovered, leases were
often abandoned, but then only after the wolf was
at the door, and few left Sillerton of their own accord, without having met with losses through the
abuse of the Game Laws—losses that had crippled
their finances for years, aye, sometimes for life.

Things, I believe, have changed, even in Sillerton.
The gentlest creature that God has created, when
driven to bay, will at least put forth an effort in
self-defence, and downtrodden, long-suffering Sillerton awoke at length from slumbers that had continued too long.

Men were at last found willing to "bell the cat,"
the bundle of sticks was repeated, joint action did
much to ameliorate the condition of the game-eaten
farmer; competition for farm leases lessened as the
channels of emigration widened, and the Juggernaut
of " Game Protection " that once rolled over a thousand Sillertons throughout Scotland, crushing, maim-
ing, grinding beneath its mighty wheels many a
noble and manly heart, many a sorrowing, despair-
ing woman, many a suffering child, lies low as that

Dagon that once fell crushed and broken before the Ark of **God.**

Well might our children ask us if such things could have been ; and well might strangers wonder whether or not the narrator of Sillerton's "burdens " was indulging in dismal romances, instead of delineating a truthful tale.

Simple truth was promised in my preface, and simple truth alone fills every chapter, and fills this chapter as well.

On facts too well known I take my stand, and defy contradiction of any kind, and from any quarter.

There are hundreds of witnesses, still in the prime of life, who could corroborate every syllable I have written here, and were I standing now in that " Auld Kirkyard," I might point to more than one grave and say—Had the whole truth been carved on these humble stones, their story might have read thus :—

" DONE TO DEATH

BY

THE LAIRD OF SILLERTON

AND

HIS GAME ! "

CHAPTER XXII.

NON-INTRUSION—THE NIGHT BEFORE THE BATTLE.

> Oh ! what a parish, a parish, a parish !
> Oh ! what a parish was drucken Dunkeld !
> They hang'd the minister, droon'd the precentor,
> Pull'd doon the steeple, and fuddl'd the bell.
> *Old Song.*

I HAVE no intention whatever of entering into the arena of Church politics that agitated Scotland for many years prior to the " forties," and which in 1843 culminated in what has been called the Disruption.

It was certainly a hardship that any patron exercising the right of patronage over a church or churches possessed the power of giving the cure of souls in the Church, where he exercised this right, to any probationer to whom the Presbytery had given a licence to preach the Gospel, and whose life had been unpointed at by the finger of scandal.

It might have indeed been urged that it was almost impossible for any one to enter the inner courts of the Church of Scotland, who was unacquainted with those marks of erudition that had been considered indispensable in completing the education of the scholar and the gentleman.

It might fairly enough have been held, that no
one of immoral character could continue to inscribe
himself a probationer of the Kirk; and it was
specially provided that the ministers of the Church
of Scotland had to be, like the Paschal lamb, without blemish.   And yet, notwithstanding such safe-
guards, it was quite possible that one might be forced
upon a congregation who was obnoxious to the great
majority of those who, in the event of his settlement
over them, must of necessity listen to his teachings,
and pay due respect to him as their spiritual adviser.

This undoubtedly was a state of things most
devoutly to be avoided, but for all that, it may have
occasionally happened.

It was, however, as unquestionably true that
sometimes, and more particularly near the period of
the Disruption, extraordinary external influences
were often brought to bear to induce Church members to ostracize a presentee, who, had no such influence been employed, would have quietly entered
into possession of the duties and emoluments of his
office without any hitch whatever.   Sillerton had
changed somewhat ecclesiastically since the days
when Louis Alexander Daff failed to put in an
appearance in his father's pulpit.   Both sire and son
had ceased from their labors, and church and school
were occupied by strangers.

The Reverend Robert Fordyce whom we have occasionally met before this in this narrative, was a quiet, unassuming man, quite satisfied with things as they were, and by no means of that volatile nature that the smallest spark of excitement might fan into flame.

Non-intrusion, therefore, did not make much progress in the parish, and, with the exception of a friendly discussion of the question in the shoemaker's workshop or the more commodious smithy, we knew remarkably little about events that were bringing some sections of the religious world to an incandescent heat.

That Mr. Fordyce would stick to the Establishment went without saying, and as the Laird would not allow a tenant to harbor even a collie dog for fear of disturbing the game, it was not at all likely that he would give much countenance to men who were wielding every influence in their power to upset the present state of things. One or two "Weeklies" came to the parish, but few conned their pages, and these few were not very favorable to the advocates of change.

A considerable revolution had, however, taken place in our educational department. The old type of dominie had passed away, and a new one had come in, lacking many of the peculiar characteristics

of the old masters, but yet full of admiration for a
system that had educated men who, in popular opinion, could walk from Aberdeen to the Wall of China
without meeting with any difficulties in the way of
unknown tongues.

These new pedagogues loved learning on its own
account, and soon began to awaken an interest in
the youth of the parish, who looked forward to the
probabilities of a college course, and perhaps a professional career beyond.

Amongst half a dozen youths then, scanning their
Horace, advancing cautiously through Greek sen-
tences, and beginning to master the difficulties of
Euclid and algebra, the burning Church question
was at all times welcome, and the arguments that
were wielded on one side or the other were all duly
weighed and gravely considered—nay, ofttimes
argued as well.

Without, however, entering into polemics; without discussing the " Veto Act " or marking out the
beauties or defects of methods that had been re-
commended to pour oil upon those troubled waters
that thereafter obtained the designation of the
" Ten Years Conflict," I shall at once come to what
may be termed the crowning point of our ecclesiastical troubles—the " Culsalmond Riot."

There were doubtless grievances connected with

the law of patronage, and there were rights belonging to Church membership that were utterly ignored,
and, to remove the one class and secure the other,
a torrent of burning zeal had rolled over the land
like a mighty stream, that half measures were as
powerless to stem as was Mrs. Partington's broom
to sweep back the waves of the Atlantic.

In Sillerton we knew that trouble was to be expected. It was not certainly known that there was
on the programme a " Riot at Culsalmond," but it
as certainly was anticipated that the settlement
there would be anything but peaceful, while it was
also pretty generally believed that the parishioners
would, on the day of settlement, be reinforced by
sympathizers who would leave no means untried to
prevent the settlement from taking place.

We shall here epitomize the circumstances of the
case. There was a vacancy in Culsalmond—a sad one
certainly—and the Presbytery of Garioch had decided to induct the Rev. Mr. Middleton, assistant to
the late incumbent, and the patron's presentee, on
the eleventh day of November, to the church and
parish of Culsalmond.

Now, seeing that the late incumbent had been
deposed for drunkenness, it might have been a wise
thing to have settled there some man of more than
ordinary ability and parts, who might have gradu-

ally undone the evil that his erring brother had contrived to do. But this, of course, was not usually a matter of interest to the patron, who, if he presented the son of an aspiring tenant to the living, conferred a lasting favor, and occasionally replenished his own depleted pocket-book.

Whatever was the cause, it was well known that the Reverend Mr. Middleton was not by any means the choice of the people. At the same time, the Presbytery were precisely in the position of a judge who had to pass sentence in accordance with existing laws. The judge had no jurisdiction over the framing of laws, but had simply to act in accordance with such as had been placed upon the Statute Book.

And so with the Presbytery of Garioch ; they were not the framers of laws, but simply the executive. The presentee of Culsalmond came before them armed with the legal documents that proved his position, and as soon as the Presbytery were satisfied as to his learning, character, and divinity, and no relevant objections were offered and sustained, there was but one course open to them. The Presbytery of Garioch therefore decided to induct Mr. Middleton on the eleventh day of November, and appointed the Reverend George Peter, of Kemnay, to preside on the occasion.

From rumors that had reached Sillerton that

the parishioners would, by fair or foul means, resist the settlement, a fellow-student and I thereupon resolved to put in an appearance at Culsalmond on that eventful November day.

Only fourteen miles or so separated us from the field of expected battle, and the day before found us, about its close, in the village of Old Rayne, where we arranged to pass the night.

Brussels, the night before Waterloo, was not more moved than that quiet village the night before the Culsalmond settlement. Alas! no Uryside Byron has arisen to perpetuate in song what then transpired.

Speedily it seemed to ooze out that two Moderates, youths certainly, had come so far to see the conflict that was likely to take place the following day. Old Rayne, unlike Sillerton, was strong in Non-intrusion sentiment, and soon its champions appeared, prepared to do battle for the great cause. I have now but a dim, a very dim recollection of the debate that followed. We two stood alone against the Rayne warriors, and did battle for the Auld Kirk as best we could.

It was, however, a hard fight, and when I think of it now, after these long years, I feel considerably surprised to think that two mere schoolboys could have held their own against the sturdy common

14

sense and genuine wit and rustic irony that were employed against them.   Truly the race is not ever to the swift, nor the battle to the strong.

Notwithstanding, however, the points we made, and the foes we routed, we began to weary of the apparently interminable nature of the contest.   Just then a happy thought seemed to strike my comrade, who was at least four or five years my senior, that it was full time that the discussion should come to a close, and that ordinary reasoning was evidently not the weapon best suited to foil our opponents.

Suiting himself, therefore, to the exigencies of the case, and the course of action he had resolved to take, he quoted from Acts that never existed, and from speeches that had never been made, to prove the stand we had taken, and the result was start-ling.   Day, date, and the *ipsissima verba*, were quoted, and as there were no documents on the spot available to rebut the statements advanced, the re-sult was very gratifying to us, and the enemies of the Kirk were smitten, "hip and thigh," like the Philistines of old before the irresistible prowess of Samson.

Some one might naïvely hint here, "And by the selfsame weapon."   Nay, gentle reader, not so; that debater made his mark where Dugald Dalgetty got his learning—in Marischal College, Aberdeen—and if any one who reads this page feels in any way anxious to know who routed the Non-intrusionists of Rayne, let him look into the chronicles of that famous seat of learning, and amongst the first bursars between 1840 and ten years thereafter he will find the name of my comrade.

Verily, had he been so inclined, he might have become Senior Wrangler of some celebrated English University, as he was undoubtedly first wrangler in the quiet village of Old Rayne on that eventful evening in November; but his lines fell to him in other places.

We were eventually left in possession of the field; the baffled disputants one by one disappeared, and we were anything but sorry that it was so.

Ten miles over country roads had made a few hours of rest peculiarly desirable, and the tension, of the tongue-and-mental struggle with the champions of Non-intrusion, had been like the last grain of sand that broke the camel's back. Supremely happy were we when we found ourselves alone; few preparations were needed to compose our weary limbs for the couch of rest; and the ringing sound of the last hobnailed boot had scarcely died away on the cobble-paved street of Old Rayne ere our heads rested on our pillows, and we were folded in the soporific arms of Morpheus.

CHAPTER XXIII.

THE CULSALMOND RIOT.

Whyles on the strong-wing'd tempest flyin,'
Tirlin' the kirks.
　　　　　　　—Address to the Deil.

NEXT morning found us ready for the road. It was a cold November morning. Bennachie had donned his white mantle, and snow-flurries, with occasional showers of hard, biting hail, greeted us as we wended our way towards the Church of Culsalmond, which stood on an eminence that tested well our staying powers, ere we conquered the " stey brae " that lay between.

If company could help our cold tramp that morning —or forenoon, we should rather say, as we intended to reach the church some time between 11 A.M. and noon—we certainly had it to our hearts' content.

From the farthest corners of the Garioch, men and youths, moved by patriotic fires, or simple curiosity, advanced in the direction of Culsalmond. The whole district—from Kintore in the southeast to parishes far beyond the Glens of Foudland—was deeply moved, the elements of combustion were already kindled, and the volcano was ready to burst forth on the heights of Culsalmond.

The day was too cold for continuous disputation; generally we trudged on in dogged silence, and in due course we reached our destination and seated ourselves on an old tombstone near the church.

So far as I can recollect, there was no house of entertainment near, but it seemed as if Scotch caution had provided against all contingencies, and that not a few were enabled, by the help of a little mountain dew, to refresh the inner man after their long and arduous walk, and to kindly temper to the shorn lambs (God save the mark!) the biting showers that still swept over hill and dale.

Deep speculation was at work as to what the Presbytery would do. But, judging from the show of legal assistance that was exhibited around the church and manse, there was no doubt but that Mr. Middleton's settlement was to be proceeded with. One thing to me seemed remarkable. The more prominent firebrands, as we learned from a parishioner, were almost all strangers. Perhaps Culsalmond was not a forcing-house for orators. Be that as it may, the parishioners, I observed, said very little.

They were pretty generally opposed to the system

that placed a clergyman over them, no matter what their feelings were; but against the presentee personally I heard not an evil word spoken, and the future abundantly proved that their action that day proceeded more from a conviction of principle than from a point of feeling.

I have said "their action," but there was little, if any action on their part that day, and what was done then to entitle the guardians of the peace to afterwards call the circumstances connected with the settlement "The Culsalmond Riot" was done principally—perhaps entirely—by outsiders.

One epithet of contempt I heard frequently applied to Mr. Middleton—"Teetaboutie." The expression awakened roars of laughter and shouts of merriment. Yet, strange to say, the expression was utterly meaningless in itself, and was simply the name of a place where the presentee once lived.

I have frequently observed that in Scottish song, sometimes the pathos depends, not so much on the sentiment expressed, as on the voice lingering sympathetically on perhaps a single word. What, after all, is in our well-known and really charming song "Robin Adair" to melt us to deepest sympathy or even tears? And yet, when the simple refrain lovingly wails forth from the very depths of the heart, few songs can be more touching.

Now, it was just so with Teetaboutie. In the word itself there was nothing. If meaning there once was, that meaning had probably died out, even before the last Druid performed his rites in the shadow of the "Maiden Stone." And yet, after hearing Teetaboutie uttered by the human voice that day in all its possible inflections—whispered by the young, rising like a slogan-yell from the capacious throats and lungs of the sturdy ploughman, and again quavering from the thin and pinched lips of men bowed down with years and hoary with age—uttered through almost a round of the clock—uttered in all the notes of the gamut, from low "G" to almost any conceivable height above, and in all its multifarious tones, expressing only deep contempt and irony, one may easily enough imagine what the effect might be.

Had the tenant of that famous place offered the writer of this the usufruct of that farm, free of rental, and insisting only that the recipient should bear the name, as all Scottish farmers do of their farms, the only reply would have been an unmitigated "No!"

Having now discussed Teetaboutie in all its bearings, I shall again take up the narrative.

It is now past eleven, and at noon precisely the members of the Garioch Presbytery intend to enter the church. The crowd, however, had no idea that such an entrance should be effected, and to carry out their purpose they closed around the church doors. No Roman soldier linked his shield more closely with that of his comrade, when assaulting some ancient wall, than "shoulder to shoulder" stood those sturdy Presbyterians who that day blockaded the church doors of Culsalmond.

At last, after some legal or ecclesiastical formalities had been attended to, the word passed along the line, if it may be so called, that the Presbytery were moving towards the church. The answer was a shout of defiance and an additional squeeze, as if some gigantic python had got another coil of his tail around you, until you began to be in doubt as to how much more pressure you could endure.

The Presbytery of Garioch now approached very close to the condensed crowd, but in this case "Tommy didn't make room for his uncle," and it looked at one time as if the blockade was not to be broken. One, however, of the County Constabulary had taken in the situation, and succeeded in carrying his point. He was a small man physically, and divesting himself of his uniform, which might have opposed his progress doorward, he somehow contrived to worm his way, without creating suspicion, to the desired spot. A quiet and unnoticed turn of the key and the blockade was broken.

The first motion of the human mass cost that constable a fractured rib, but beyond a sharp cry of pain we knew nothing. We were sensible of a slow grinding motion that was in unceasing progress; we faced sometimes the gable of the church and sometimes the everlasting hills; we were conscious of a compressive force that was almost unbearable; we had no power whatever to alter, in the very slightest degree, the course we were involuntarily taking, but we saw and felt that we were approaching slowly, but surely, the open door.

With hands high overhead, and with feet innocent of contact with the gravel or grass that lay beneath them, that door was reached. That particular moment, amidst all my subsequent experiences and wanderings, has never been forgotten. If two hundred pounds upon the square inch was what I endured before, there were at least a thousand as I slowly rolled past one of the doorposts.

Not more swiftly does the tensioned string regain its normal condition when the tension ceases, than my corporation came back to its original form. I seemed to shoot forward as if an old resuscitated catapult had propelled me.

But, in fact, there was a double propulsion. The

one was produced by a species of vacuum in front, and the propelling power behind; the other sprang from that principle of love of life that stimulates many of the forces of the human mind. But, to explain: no sooner was I within the door than a sound struck on my ear that precluded all other sounds whatever.

That there was a perfect pandemonium there, may go without saying. The roar of a flooded cata-ract was nothing in comparison to the mingled sounds that were heard within that building. And yet the distinct crack of a beam overhead was louder still.

With the agility of youth, stimulated by the spur of fear, the top of a pew was reached, a few bounds left the cracked and still cracking gallery behind, and with a careful eye to the possibilities of falling stars and things of that sort, I speedily found my-self in a window, and considered that I was as secure from the evil chances of war, as any one might well be while he remained under that roof.

From my perch I could now look with some equanimity upon things transpiring about me. I am not aware whether or not the Moderator ever ascended the pulpit steps. It would have been an act of supreme folly to have even attempted such a thing, as both stair and pulpit were already occupied to repletion, and as the uproar that raged on every side would have precluded the possibility of any human voice being heard, were it loud as that of an African lion.

Patiently, very patiently, the members of Presbytery kept their usual places beside the pulpit foot. Nor was this an easy or desirable task. The ceaseless roar of angry and determined men, irritated the more by their failure to debar the clergy from the church, was not the only disturbing element there, but pieces of wood, of stone, and of lime were being thrown in every direction throughout the building.

And well did the Presbytery of Garioch stand the test. There might have been differences of opinion as to the goodness of their cause ; there was but one with respect to their bearing under such peculiarly trying circumstances, and that was one of general admiration. Personally, I was prejudiced in favor of our clergy, but I could not look that day upon their calm, determined bearing without thinking of their Covenanting forefathers preaching to their scattered followers amidst the mosses and moors of troubled Scotland, where the sabres of Claverhouse's dragoons might at any moment have ended both preaching and life together.

Such, thought I, were our fathers once, and such

are their sons now. After waiting for a considerable time for a patient hearing, the members of
Presbytery withdrew in a body from the building,
and sought the quieter rooms of the neighboring
manse, where the settlement of the presentee was
legally and ecclesiastically consummated.

The storm that raged, however, within the walls
of the church was not hushed to rest when the
clergy left it. "Holy Willie's Prayer" was given
from the pulpit by special request; ribald songs
were sung by the excited and sometimes inebriated
ploughmen ; the bell never ceased its jowl until the
shades of evening were coming down upon the
church and churchyard, and not until almost all
the chief actors had left the manse for their comparatively distant homes, did the revellers pause in
their weird-like work, did the smoke of hundreds
of pipes cease to roll forth from the shattered and
glassless windows of the now dilapidated building,
and did that old bell abandon a lugubrious refrain
that has never been rung again, and we sincerely
hope may never again,on the world-renowned heights
of Culsalmond.

A few days afterwards I attended a wedding in
the neighborhood of Sillerton, where the Reverend
Robert Fordyce officiated. It was, of course, well
known that he had been at Culsalmond as a member

of the Presbytery, and that while on his way home the day following, and not very far from the village, some slight accident happened to the horse, and, in consequence, minister, man, and vehicle got landed in the ditch.

A friendly parishioner and his ploughman who witnessed the accident kindly came to the rescue, and, with some little difficulty, all were, like John Gilpin's hat and wig, soon again on the road. The father of the bride was somewhat dull of hearing, but on this occasion he seemed duller than usual. The fact was that the old farmer meant to quiz the minister and succeeded. Three times I heard the question put, " Far war ye comin' frae, minister, the ither day fin yer beastie fell i' the ditch ? " As often the answer came, but in rather subdued tones. The fourth " speerin' " brought a reply that was heard all over the room, " From Culsalmond, sir ! from Culsalmond."

The smothered titter that rippled through the well-filled apartment showed that the shot had told, and the good-natured host, showing only a merry twinkle in his eye, did not pursue the conversation.

Another clerical friend of mine in after years was not so reticent as to things that transpired at the riot, and more than once induced me to tell the story.

I had seen him leave the manse of Culsalmond on

that eventful evening, and, as a number of rustics attempted to bar his way along Her Majesty's high-way, he leapt his horse into a turnip field. Here he was rather closely followed for some distance by the rabble, but, being well mounted, he got a slight distance ahead, and at last saw his way clear to the highway again. Wheeling his panting nag towards his pursuers, he lifted his hat, made a profound salaam, and rode away. This was too much for his tormentors. One cheer was raised, and the chase ended.

This story he delighted to repeat long years afterwards, and that exciting ride through that stiff turnip-field gave him, in its remembrance, more delight than the recollections of the best sermon he had ever preached. Such are we all; such is human nature everywhere.

I saw the carriage of an aristocratic member of Presbytery also leave the manse under difficulties. A shower of something harder and larger than hailstones damaged considerably the "Dalrymple Arms" on the well varnished panels, but the equanimity of the occupant was in no way disturbed. In conversation afterwards the gallant baronet explained that an ordinary shower of stones was not likely to intimidate a man who had lived for years with only a sheet of gray paper between him and the infernal region.

In the witness-box some short time afterwards, the undaunted elder further explained, that he had spent several years of his life in latitudes where volcanic eruptions were almost of daily occurrence.

Before closing this chapter I cannot fail to remark the peculiar tendency of the Scottish mind to express its feelings in verse under circumstances of an exciting nature. The several ecclesiastical movements that preceded the Disruption of 1843 seemed to arouse this tendency to action.

I have in my possession several specimens of what were once called "Culsalmond Psalms," and they exhibit no small amount of fire and sarcastic humor. I presume, however, that, as in the case of the letters of Junius, the same remark as to the authorship may be repeated—*Stat nominis umbra.*

In my own case, while still in my teens, I was once guilty of a slight act of indiscretion in turning into rude verse the ludicrous adventure of a love-sick well-known breeder of Aberdeenshire cattle. It was never intended that the little "jeu de esprit" should go further than the dining-room table, but the retentive memory of a listener immortalized what should have been committed to oblivion. Next market day, the song was said and sung through the ancient burgh of Inverurie.

Nor was it cast as a waif upon the world, for the paternity was willingly owned by one who that day reaped a golden harvest from its sale.

I can recall still the sturdy upper-country poet, opening his musical campaign on the forenoon of a market day. Clad in home-spun, the stalwart Glen-livat man tossed the loose end of his plaid over his shoulder, and, stepping forward, half sung, half recited rhymes such as the following :—

> " I'm John Milne frae Livat's glen ;
> I wrat it doon wi' my ain pen.
> Over the mountains, over the main,
> Ridin' thro' France, and gallopin' thro' Spain :
> Skippin' the mountains like a craw,
> And o'er the hills to Americaa ! "

Such was the poet who claimed my verses, and sold them, too. Unlike the great Roman Virgil, I left the perpetrator of "petty larceny" to enjoy his gold and his laurels in peace, but sometimes in after years, when I have heard a verse or two of my effu-sion quoted, doubtless a very sinister smile may have played around my lips.

It is possible that even, now after so many years have come and gone, some old friend of the Garioch Presbytery may read these lines, and, thinking of little links that connected him with those troublous and stormy times, smile also, and half own that there were more Johnny Milnes in the world than one, more shadows that will remain shadows to the end.

History but repeats itself, and even with regard to the Culsalmond Psalms, we may again quote the saying— *Stat nominis umbra!*

15

CHAPTER XXIV.

LAST DAYS AT SCHOOL.

And will it breathe into him all the zeal,
That candidates for such a prize should feel,
To take the lead and be the foremost still
In all true worth and literary skill ?
—COWPER.

WITH the close of events narrated in the last chapter, the ecclesiastical battles of the Garioch ceased, so far at least as we were concerned, and the Latinists of Sillerton had settled down to what boys now would call a "steady grind."

Time was creeping on, and we were approaching that age when we were expected to push our fortune on a wider field than in the parish school. It was, indeed, no child's play that lay before us now.

By "us," I mean half a dozen youths, not yet claiming the sweet sixteen, but closely approaching it, and grinding up, for all they were worth, the different branches of study that might land them amongst the list of prizemen, who by and by would reap the laurels of the annual competition at the two Aberdeen Universities, then two in everything but divinity, now happily blended into one noble institution, able and willing to educate the aspiring youth of the North.

The subjects on which the competitors would be examined were simply two, namely, the rendering of English into Latin, and vice versa, or the rendering of Latin into English, or as we called it, "version and translation." To become proficient in these two subjects required no small amount of self-denial and study.

We had a teacher fresh from academic halls himself, and burning to send youths to the competition, who, in winning honors to themselves, would reflect a portion of that honor upon their teacher. We were then ably coached. The usual hour for school was ten, but the teacher and Latinists met at nine, so as to have a good hour of higher education, without those interruptions which were likely to occur when the ordinary scholars began the work of the day.

Every morning a version, as it was called, was given out, while the one of the day before was examined and duly rated. How anxiously we listened to the reading of the daily record!

Men waiting to hear the decision of a jury that

chained them or set them free, were not more anxious than we were, and when the name came with the coveted *Sine errore*, this was one of the happiest moments of our life.

But, after all, was this not a foreshadowing of many a scene of after-life, where we, or such as we, must needs be judged? Are there not times when the malicious efforts of enemies may conspire to materialize a cloud around us ; when treacherous lips will whisper doubtings softly to the ear, that would not dare to speak them out manfully, face to face ; when appearances that in themselves meant little or nothing were so distorted and twisted by diabolical manipulation as to almost prove anything whatever ; and yet, at length, when the vile attempt has broken down, when the clouds of cruel suspicion have "rolled by," when they who may have been led to doubt us, have found cause to give a purer and holier judgment—then the verdict of our boyhood's teacher is again repeated, and to our ears comes once again the pleasing judgment—*Sine errore.*

And looking beyond self, there are few who have not made some "maxies" in the version of life. Ah ! when an erring brother or maybe sister is being weighed, let, then, our gentler sympathies go forth through that indescribable feeling that links one heart to another—go forth to help the weak to weigh down the beam on mercy's side. Such may be like bread cast upon the waters, that shall yet be found again, even though after many days.

And when our own last account is rendered, may errors, failings, weaknesses, transgressions all be blotted out, and through the merits of One who once said—nay, often said—"Though your sins be like scarlet they shall be as white as snow," and who, though now exalted, feels as we feel, in the possession of a nature the same as ours. Then may our record, with all its imperfections, be accepted through His merits alone, and over the blurred and obliterated evidences of much shortcoming, the verdict be clearly and distinctly written—*Sine errore.*

These were certainly anxious and hard times. With us, truly, there was no royal road to the grand truths contained in the writings of ancient Greece and Rome. The Latin Rudiments, from title-page to finis; Melvin's Grammar, with its hundreds of lines of Latin hexameters ; Greek grammars, Cæsar, Virgil, Horace, Xenophon, and, as a species of alterative, arithmetic, algebra, and geometry thrown in —this was the "bill of fare" on which the choice youths of Sillerton were encouraged to try their mental teeth. Nor did we flinch from the ordeal.

We were well coached, as stated before. The master had himself travelled over the same road.

He knew every step of the way, and we never lacked encouragement to press on—his motto and ours being ever "Excelsior." As an example of the judicious treatment we received, I shall recount an experience of my own in the earlier stages of our Latinity.

I had mastered a few hundred lines of Melvin's hexameters without any extraordinary difficulties, and to the satisfaction of the master, when suddenly a change—a change for the worse—came over me. My memory seemed to fail; the lines, usually so easily committed, would scarcely limp along; and lessons generally were, without doubt, a sad failure. I must have looked unhappy, but the teacher's countenance expressed despair. He quietly took me aside, asked what was the matter, and questioned me with evident anxiety if I really had lost my interest in classical studies, lost my senses, lost anything that should not have been lost.

I owned up at once. Young George Washington, when he carved the paternal cherry tree without the paternal permission, was not more candid than I. I had, unfortunately—very unfortunately—laid my hands upon one of Jane Porter's novels—"Thaddeus of Warsaw"—and from that ill-fated moment no line of Melvin's Grammar could find a resting-place in my memory.

I received there and then, and most kindly too, a holiday sufficiently long to enable me to finish my story; I received also at the same time some very excellent advice which I have never since forgotten. In due course the romance speedily passed away; back came the hexameters in all their beauty and smooth-ness; and the beam of satisfaction that played over the teacher's face as he listened to the wisdom of the old stern grammarian (known by the nickname of "Old Grim") repeated carefully and correctly by the lips of his pupil, showed clearly that our golden age had again returned.

Summer was now amongst the things of the past, the golden sheaves of autumn had all been stored away in the huge cornstacks that gladdened the farmers' hearts, and adorned their courtyards. The little boys and girls of the village were looking forward anxiously to the next moon to enjoy the rustic game of "hide and seek" amongst the lights and shadows that would be found there; but, alas! there was no "hide and seek" in store for the busy Latinists.

Probably we thought and said, too, with a sigh, "Every dog has its day," and we may have had ours also among the cornstacks. "Hide and seek" was unquestionably a fascinating game even when played by boys, but when the challenge came, "Boys and girls come out to play," its charms were increased a thousand-fold.

It is asserted by scientists that, on even a calm ocean, there is an attraction between vessels lying near each other, that may bring them into dangerous proximity, nay, into perilous contact. And so, in the sweet game of "hide and seek," how often did one find himself, in the friendly shadow of the cornstacks, near some youthful maiden, whose sums he had often worked out for her, and whose hand he was, in consequence, permitted to gently press, away from the gairy and tell-tale moonbeams.

Ah! much do I fear, were the truth told, that Thaddeus of Warsaw was not the only disturbing influence that crept into the parish school to cripple our hexameters; there were little episodes of romance amidst even our school-days that would cross our paths to interfere at times with sterner duties, and when I think of it, the reciprocating squeeze of a gentle hand, or the kindly blink of a loving eye, did sometimes make sad havoc in our ranks.

I fear, also, that in these cases we were not quite so candid as when the Polish patriot was at fault; it would have taken more than thumbscrews to make us own to the douce dominie that some bonnie Jean had come between us and our allotted tasks; we were willing to stand unlimited chaffing in such a cause; the secret, after all, was our own, and were we not acting up to the advice of our great bard, and who knew better?—" And keep aye something to yoursell, ye dinna tell to ony."

The autumn games were then not for us, and when we returned to school, after our six weeks of holidays, it was only to say, "Good-bye," and to receive credentials to one or other of the Grammar Schools, that in Old or New Aberdeen prepared youths for the approaching competition. This course was not always adopted. Boys often remained at the parish school to the very last; but many sought the Grammar School, as affording a wider arena, where the classical athlete could find a larger number of competitors with whom to measure his own strength and prowess.

My own departure from home was accompanied with more than one trial. Leaving home with all its agreeable associations, and generally, for the first time, is far from pleasant. Looking forward to the dandy jacket of a smart "middy," or even to a month's fishing among the lochs and tarns of the great Grampian range, makes home-leaving anything but painful, but in our case, there was no play in prospect, but only good stern work before us; the midnight oil must needs be burned; our lottery was not "all prizes and no blanks;" the prizes were indeed only for a few, and when the short roll of the successful competitors should be called, at least four-fifths of the crowd would return in disappointment to their homes. Many of these last, however, would enter the classes with their more fortunate companions, but to not a few this would be denied.

Prior to the competition I ranked myself among this number. I had been given to understand that my entering the college depended entirely on my proving a successful competitor. Whether it was wise or otherwise to give such an assurance may be difficult to determine. Much might be said on both sides. Doubtless what was done was done for the best, and at all events, in the present case, while it hinted at the painful consequences of defeat, it neither weakened hand nor heart in preparing for the fray.

My father, with commendable caution, had, unknown to any member of the family, procured for me the promise of a presentation bursary, in the event of my defeat at the competition, but with commendable pride he much preferred a bursary won by merit alone. Whether or not he was gratified in this, we shall see hereafter. Often have I burned the midnight oil, but never more unremittingly and faithfully than then ; often have I seen the rising sun peep in at the attic window to startle eyes that had not yet tasted sleep, but there was an intenseness in the work done then, that was never felt afterwards in the same ratio.

There was then an issue at stake that might cast sunshine or shadow over a whole lifetime—an issue that, in its intensity, never seemed to be approached in after years.

My own fate seemed to lie within the compass of my own hands, and like the youthful warrior who buckled on for the first time, his maiden sword, to me victory and defeat seemed to poise upon a level beam.

I knew that all Sillerton stood on tiptoe of expectation; the genial, anxious dominie never failed to send messages of encouragement and good cheer; and round the family hearth I well knew that kindly hearts felt the deepest sympathy in all my experiences, and never ceased to long and pray earnestly for a "Godspeed."

And thus the weeks passed by; the versions approached in correctness the models that were day by day placed before us, till *sine errore* became the rule instead of being the exception. And so also with other studies.

We were approaching the end very perceptibly, and as the rector closed his book on the Saturday preceding the great day of competition, I can almost recall his parting bow before dismissing us, and hear again the fervent wish that we might distinguish ourselves in the approaching classic tournament, and shed fresh lustre, not only upon ourselves, but upon the Grammar School of Old Aberdeen, nay, upon its rector as well.

Well might we have all replied, prayerfully, fervently, humbly, " So mote it be."

CHAPTER XXV.

THE CONCLUSION—THE COMPETITION AND THE GOWN.

He that no more must say, is listened more
  Than they whom youth and ease have taught to gloze ;
More are men's ends mark'd, than their lives before ·
  The setting sun, and music at the close,
As the last taste of sweets is sweetest last ;
Writ in remembrance, more than things long past.
  —*Richard II.*

On a bleak morning near the end of October, between the year 1840 and a decade later, somewhat over one hundred and fifty competitors sat down in the long room of King's College, to test their skill in an academic tourney, that had, after all, but a few prizes to offer, and where also, the great majority would feel like the unhorsed knights of old, when sword and lance both lay shivered on the ground.

No roll was called, for the competition was open to Scotland, or, for that matter, to the world at large; and had a "heathen Chinee" and a fur-clad Esquimaux presented themselves at that table, they would have found a place, and, provided their Latinity was up to the mark, they had as good a chance of success as the Scottish youth who had studied his classics in some of the famous Grammar Schools of the north.

Two or three professors were on duty. Poor little Tulloch went limping round the room, as anxious and fidgety as if he were one of the competitors himself; Greek "Habby," though old and frail, still held his own, and looked as if, when in his prime, he would have been more likely to have proved the victor in an old-time wrestling match than to win the poet's crown at the Olympic games.

And last, though not least, came burly Prosody, as we always called our Professor of Humanity. We believed, indeed, that Prosody would rather have arrayed himself in a Roman toga than encase his massive limbs in the more artificial habiliments of a modern Scot. I never looked at him without dreaming of Cicero, and it was generally believed, at least amongst the "Bageants," that Prosody thought in Latin hexameters.

The version, as it was called, was slowly dictated, and thereafter we all bent ourselves resolutely to our task. The only book allowed us was the ordinary Latin dictionary, and keen eyes watched that no other tome or notes of any kind were used. The hours wore on in profound stillness, broken only by the peculiar sound that a hundred and fifty pens, operating all at the same time, make upon a hundred and fifty sheets of paper.

A change of watchmen comes, and as the guard is relieved in comes the good old Dr. Hercules Scott, with a smile upon his kindly face that told as plainly as so many words, that he personally would be glad could we all be first bursars or prizemen. Dr. Fyfe follows trippingly, and walks along with as little apparent interest as if he would gladly boil down all the Latin and mathematics in the universe in one of his own retorts.

And last glides in, for all the world like a feline, the erudite Professor of Natural Philosophy. Smooth-tongued was he as "Oily Gammon" himself, but, a stranger to our northland ways, he never gained the students' hearts, and never awoke anything more than a hiss in after-days, when professors and students sought the Public Hall on occasions of discipline.

There were more professors present than those mentioned, but I have sketched, very roughly it may be, at least the principal figures.

And so the day wears on. Time was called at last, and each candidate, after placing a certain number on his exercise and the same number and his name on a coupon attached, separated the two and placed the pieces in different boxes.

This closed the first day's work—in fact, the more important part of the competition—as the translation of Latin into English was not considered by any means so drastic a test of mental capacity, as the turning of English into choice Ciceronian Latin.

Next day found us at our post again, with the same guard mounted over us, and when the hours for work were exhausted time was again called, the same boxing operation took place as on the day previous, and we, alone or in small groups, wended our ways to our respective places of abode, to go over our work again in the quiet of our own rooms. to mark what errors we had made, if any, and to calculate our chances of success.

The few days that intervened between the competition days and that on which the list of prizemen or bursars would be published in the Public Hall of the College dragged very wearily along. I had examined and re-examined every word and line and sentence; idioms had all been thoroughly looked into ; genders of nouns, conjugations of verbs, and rules of syntax had all been applied as a line and plummet to the double exercise, and I felt reasonably satisfied with what I had done.

The schoolmaster of Sillerton was duly communicated with and his opinion requested. His reply came—We of Sillerton were pretty equally matched, so far as talents or scholarship went, but in nervous susceptibility we were indeed very different. The strain had proved too much for my comrades; they had simply lost their heads, and in consequence errors had crept in—errors that might, nay, that certainly would, count heavily against them.

I alone seemed likely to be successful: in my exercises there were no maxies—no glaring errors; there was, in one or two places, room for improvement, but taking one thing with another, the chances of success were on my side. Mark, "chances" only. The kindly teacher felt very confident, as he afterwards told me, but he feared to raise my hopes too high, lest I might feel disappointment the more bitterly should I have already almost anticipated the joys of triumph.

At last the day—the eventful day—arrived. Accompanied by my father, who had come from Sillerton that morning with a few others equally interested, I wended my way from New to Old Aberdeen, past the canal bridge, beneath which then passed many a barge laden with the produce of the Garioch and Buchan districts; past the Red Lion of famous memory, with the Latin motto, *Serva jugum*, painted boldly upon its capacious signboard,

16

and which all students, from time immemorial, persisted in translating, "Hand round the jug "— past this famous hostelry, I said, until, passing under the lofty and elegant granite crown that distinguishes the well-known and ancient seat of learning, we entered the great square, which we found crowded by hundreds, attracted thither by a motive the same as that which had drawn ourselves.

A few anxious and restless moments pass; then the old bell clangs loudly from a neighboring tower; the massive doors are thrown open, and we rush in, as if every man and boy among us firmly believed in the adage, "Deil tak' the hindmost."

There, in a railed-in dais, clothed in silken gowns, and wearing shiny hats, sat the members of the Senatus Academicus, prepared to disclose the secrets that were contained in a roll that lay on the book-board before them.

Soon every sound was hushed in expectation of the approaching dénouement, and I doubt not every competitor felt much as a culprit does, as the jury-men file into the room, and the foreman stands ready to make known the decision of the twelve men— "good and true."

The sacrist, armed with the symbol of authority, approaches the dais, and laying the sceptre upon the table, steps aside to await the issue of events. There is still a moment's pause, and then a whisper passes along the professorial line, and seems particularly directed to the centre figure of the group.

I at once recognize a very aged man, whom I had observed while we were waiting outside, approaching the great hall door, leaning on the arm of a lady, who there left him in the care of one of the College officials.

This I learned afterwards to be Principal Jack, now, of course, relieved from duty, except, perhaps, when his venerable appearance and great age would tend to add additional dignity to a professorial meeting. I observed also at a glance that the old Principal was blind.

As he rose slowly to his feet, the other members of the Senatus rose; the roll of names was placed in the old man's hands, and the Professor standing next to him seemed ready to whisper each name, as it came in order of merit, to the Principal's ear. I need not say how awful was the silence now.

At last, at last it was broken; the whispered name came in measured, yet in tremulous tones from the old Principal's lips, and one shout of triumph rose "loud and long" from the friends and relatives of the successful first bursar, who now stepped forward at the beck of the sacrist to a place of honor nearer the Professorial line.

Another and another name is called, and my hopes are beginning to sink low. Ten or eleven names have been called, and yet Sillerton is unrepresented amongst the beaming line of happy faces now lifted immeasurably above all the rest. The twelfth name comes. Can it be possible? Can I be deceived? Could there be another of the same name? No major, no minor is appended.

A hearty shout greets my victory; a dozen friendly hands push me forward, and Donald Andrew, of Sillerton, stands amongst the acclaimed bursars of King's College and University of Aberdeen.

Little more remains to be told. The same afternoon my delighted father had me arrayed in cap and gown in one of the famous clothing establishments of Bon-Accord.

I would have fain taken a run to Sillerton to spend a quiet day at home, and in truth I needed it, and perhaps to enjoy the congratulations of my friends and acquaintances there, but this might not be. There was no railroad in those days to Sillerton, and matriculation day was close at hand. I decided to remain, and that evening I saw my father off on the old " Defiance " mail-coach.

" Good-bye, Donald, and God bless you," said the old man, cheerily, in a dialect learned in school on the banks of the Spey, learned as Sillerton boys learned their Latin and Greek, and which still, on occasions, even after the lapse of so many years, I sometimes seem to hear as the softened echo of a familiar voice gently thrown back from a distant hill. "Wherever you are," he said, "never forget that you are a gentleman."

As the driver gathered together the reins in his hand, and the scarlet-coated guard gave the last signal on his official horn that Her Majesty's "Defiance" was ready to start on its journey northward, he had only time to add, "I will remember you kindly to the schoolmaster, and to your other friends in Sillerton, nor will I forget to tell all at home that you looked right well in your King's College Cap and Gown."

THE END.